Sovereign

Part Two of the Irdesi Empire Series

By
Addison Cain

Chapter 1

Waves breaking against rocks and the crisp rumble of vast water stole through dreams of ripping metal and hissing gasses. It was not easy to wake, to find that each breath smelled slightly of salt and not of stale recycled atmosphere.

Brightness muddled sight when lashes parted and Sigil found the proverbial vision of heaven.

The side of her face pressed to cloth the same color as Que's flesh. Facing open gates of glass that offered blue sky, she felt nothing but the torments of hell. A growing sob crushed her heart, and she shut her eyes so tight her skull ached.

Long ago, before her name was Quinn, she had cried like that—like a dying animal. Alone, cut off from sentient life after she'd eaten the last of her attackers on that wild world she'd crashed into as a child. There she'd howled pitifully after ages of solitude.

That same horrible emptiness hollowed her out now.

The only life that mattered to her was lost.

There was no Que to guide her. She'd been deserted, left in a palatial room with walls that glowed as if carved from opal. There was no Que because his battered head had been cut off and placed in a cryobox.

There was no Que because she had utterly failed him.

This was all her fault.

Her cries distorted into muffled screams against the soft foreign mattress, each breath more painful than any blow she'd ever taken. Howls built until she could hardly breathe, until the pressure behind her eyes brought piercing pain to her skull.

Blood dripped from her nostrils. She ignored it. After all, the covers had already grown damp from her outburst. The whole of that great bed may as well have been broken glass.

Quinn bawled until there were no more tears.

The subsequent exhausted numbness deadened a bit of the grief.

Staring dumbly out those huge open doors to a balcony drenched in sun, she willed her heart to stop beating.

Her body denied her. Sleep came instead.

The next time she woke, what had been almost blinding whiteness had altered to soft gold sunlight. Aching as if she'd slept too long, hungry, confused, she pressed up from the vast bed.

Her wrists were circled by etched gold, the bracelets' decoration of ancient design jingled when she moved. Her nails had been shaped, cleaned. There was no crust of dried blood on her face or grainy remnants of salty tear stains on her cheeks. Someone had cleaned her, dressed her.

Ignoring the odd decoration, disinterested in ornamentation, she untangled her legs from the pleated, translucent gown knotted at her throat and stood.

The ground was warm as if it had been heated by sunlight, her feet, painted gold, a similar shade.

Stiff, stepping toward the nearest gaping view, all that was to be seen was ocean. Vast, endless turquoise lapped at the side of the rounded cliff her gilded cage had been carved into. There was nothing to swim to, no sign of hovercraft or spaceship, only birds circling, and water creatures playing near the milder break.

The single interior door was the only other available route.

There was no electric panel or vid display to help her navigate its unbolting, only an archaic lever. Under her fingertips, ancient mechanics etched into the wood gave way when she pressed down.

The door was not locked.

Sliding it open, she found a circular anteroom as bizarre as anyone might imagine. The visual curio was segmented into quadrants depicting the seasons of old Earth. She was standing in Summer, gazing up to find a fresco painted on the ceiling above her—cartwheeling gods from a culture she did not know smiled down in their glory.

In the center of the room, a fountain spouted crystal clear water, but that was not what drew her attention. It was the walls of gilded mirrors and the stranger reflected in them. Gone were the dyed lavender eyes, and in their place the icy vibrancy of a glacier. Gone was the sheared skull. Instead, waves hung past her waist. All the pigments Quinn had used to alter her hair into any shade but her own had been leached away, displaying the ethereal brilliance of pale silvery blonde—a shade she had not seen herself since she was a child.

She touched the cool glass.

Nothing looked familiar. The woman reflected was a ghost, an alien.

"Is it so strange?"

Red-rimmed eyes cut to the reflection across the room. She offered the smallest of nods, her attention returning to her image.

No sound accompanied his approach, only the growing size of the uniformed male dwarfing her figure in the mirror. Sovereign was so much taller, boasting a body that spoke of great strength, while her pale reflection was lissome, a wraith with a face of misery and disorientation.

Where she was fragmented, he radiated wholeness, authority.

Eyes far deeper than the ocean she'd glimpsed from the window tracked over her appearance, full of that same unwelcome tenderness she had first seen years ago.

He asked, "Is there any lingering pain?"

Voice low and lifeless, she pointed to her heart. "Here."

Tears slipped over her cheeks, collecting at her chin to fall on the floor. "Where have you brought me?"

"Somewhere secure. A palace where you can find rest." Voice gentle, mind calm, Sovereign added, "There was a great deal of damage to your brain from the psionic burst that even your rapid healing could not fully counter. You've been asleep for forty-seven years. During that time there were operations, gene therapy, augmentation."

Large eyes burned, filling with hate. "Trying to rectify the mistake you made while I was in gestation?"

The man reached out and brushed the back of his fingers down her long tangle of silvery hair.

"Yes."

She could sense his intention. He was goading her on purpose, testing to see how close she might be to losing control. But he was not completely false. She could feel the oddest heat against the left side of her skull. They *had* put something inside her. "It's a pity you could not cut out my memory too."

His emotions projected agreement, though Sovereign did not voice his opinion aloud. "The psionic centers of your brain have been fitted with suppression technology that will disperse overload. With practice, tailored psionic ability will be available to you now."

Looking to the warming line atop her skull, she imagined where a long circular scar would have developed had she been human. Unimpressed, numb, she muttered, "I have never slept so long... It doesn't feel as if so much time has passed."

Sovereign's fingertips tucked a lock of hair behind her ear, his voice thick with sentiment. "I felt every hour."

She would feel every last painful crawling hour without her companion, and that thought was awful. "There is no sort of life worth living without Que."

The heat of his hand settled on her shoulder, a thumb dipping under her hair to gently stroke her nape. "I would never have killed him. I want you to know that. I would never have willingly given you such pain."

The sincerity of the Emperor's soft spoken words scorched her. Visibly cringing, wanting to dump the blame at his feet, she accused him of his greater slight. "You should have let me die."

"Quinn did die. Sigil was reborn—the past burned away."

Forlorn, her voice broke. "I don't want to be Sigil..."

Poisoned words were softly offered. "Do you want to be Quinn without Que?"

It felt as if he'd ripped straight through her ribcage. As if Sovereign brutally squeezed her heart as she'd once pulverized Drinta's. "No." Her face contorted into one of pain. "Quinn could never survive without him."

The rich compulsion in his voice made the answer seem so simple. "Then they both must be mourned and set aside. As it is now, you have so many reasons to live." He applied more pressure, parting her vertebrae gently. Sovereign purposefully fostered her comfort until the female's shoulders relaxed. "All these years, your Brothers have kept vigil. All the love you seek awaits your recognition."

"Had I the energy, I would kill you, Sovereign. I would move room by room through wherever you've stashed me, slaughtering every remnant of Project Cataclysm that crossed my path."

A gracious smile was offered, Sovereign seemingly pleased with her threats. "I have a gift for you, something that will require a gentle hand." He turned toward the segment of Winter. "Come forward, child."

Another mirror displayed the shy flash of yellow scales. The boy, her Tessan boy she'd left in the cryotube on Pax, ambled nervously forward.

From his anxious expression, he'd heard her threats and openly feared her.

Guilt found a way to worm through her grief. Memories of Pax, of her outburst... of all the life she'd squelched bubbled up.

"The boy has been in full cryo, waiting for you to wake and decide his fate." Sovereign gestured for the child to come closer.

Mincing steps of a born slave obeyed the summons, his obvious terror softening the horrified expression on Sigil's face.

She took the smallest step toward the Emperor, using his body as if to shield the child from herself. "Do you know me, boy?"

There was no answer. The little one was frightened, more than unsure, his tail making little flicks behind him against the cool Winter floor.

Her imaginings for him had been simple: a warm home in an outlying Tessan colony where fresh life was needed. Not this.

The young male looked up at her and she sensed what he truly desired. He wanted his mother.

And Sigil had killed her… had been the cause of the deaths of tens of thousands on Pax.

"The Imperial Consort asked you a question, Jerla." That was not a tone Sigil had ever heard Sovereign employ. It was the tenor one used to guide children. It was a voice of reason and comfort.

The Tessan child shook his head no.

Grief of another sort welled until Sigil felt pinpricks behind her eyes. "I know you, Jerla, son of the slave Ragi." Sovereign dared to slip an arm around her as she spoke, as if to restrain her, to hold her, all the while his terrible mind echoing feelings of reassurance while she spoke. "I have known you since you were birthed. I was the one who hid billop eggs near your sleeping mat when you were good."

His vertical eyelids blinked, the child excited by the mention of his favorite treat. "I liked that game."

"So did I."

Another touch from the Emperor, gentle fingers threaded into her hair. Sigil wanted to retaliate, to shove him off, but was too busy staring at the child.

She forced the smallest of smiles. "Have you been happy since you woke?"

Those shining black eyes blinked at her, the male too young to understand. "I get to eat whenever I am hungry."

A slave's version of bliss.

"When I was only a little older than you, I was trapped on a world alone for many years, very hungry."

Innocent, Jerla asked, "Why?"

Sigil's smile faded, sadness returning. "My ship was shot down by bad men. Do you know the difference between bad men and good men?"

How could he? All he had ever known was Pax, drudgery, and neglect. Even so, Jerla nodded in agreement.

"I killed all of those men and lived in the ruins of their outpost until a stranger found me… a good man. The first I had ever met."

The boy's tale swished in interest at her tale. "How did you know he was good?"

Sigil swallowed. "He was the opposite of me in every way."

"You were not good?"

"No," Sigil shook her head, expression grim. "I was not good."

Fear crept into those pitch eyes again.

Sovereign held her tighter, a warning that she must desist from her path. "And she seeks to atone, Jerla. That is why she saved you from the destruction of Pax."

That is not why she had saved him, but Sigil was not going to damage the friendless thing further.

Gentleness leached from Sovereign's voice, replaced with deep-voiced authority. "Thank her quickly, Jerla. The Imperial Consort requires rest."

Shifting foot to foot, his bare little toes clicking on the stone floor, Jerla looked unsure. "Thanks."

Already pulling Sigil toward the Spring segment of the circular anteroom, Sovereign instructed, "Off with you now. You can play with her when she is feeling better."

Where the Tessan child went, Sigil did not see. She was simply glad he was gone. It had been too much, she was too empty, and so she let Sovereign lead her through an open arch into another room.

The sleeping chamber had been Summer, but the dining hall—walls laden with edible growing things and latticed windows overlooking that same endless sea—was clearly Spring.

Food already waited on the table, the dishes beyond Sigil's experience to recognize. Placed in a chair, Sovereign was wise enough to only hand her water. "What made you chose that child over all the young ones on Pax?"

She didn't answer. Cup at her lips, she swallowed, eyes locked on a round deep purple fruit growing nearby.

"That is a mangosteen. According to old Earth legend, inside the shell is something soft that tastes of extinct berries. It is an extreme rarity in these times."

Resigned, Sigil sighed. "With all your planets, you could find a climate to host forests of any fancy fruit you wanted."

"Ecosystems, like politics, are tricky things. New plant life can unbalance whole worlds in less than one human generation."

"So can Irdesian forced Conversion."

Sovereign had the gall to laugh. "True." Reaching past her, he plucked a mangosteen as if the table before him was not already ripe with food.

There was an art to opening the fruit, to revealing the soft pale flesh hidden behind its thick shell. He showed her this before offering a piece. "Here."

The odd segment smelt of nula milk, a thing she'd once craved. "No."

Shrugging, Sovereign took the flesh and ate it, leaning back in his chair to watch his female pretend she was not crying. "You have to eat to stay strong. You need to eat so you might guide Jerla's path."

"He doesn't belong amongst humans."

"Why? They have shown him more care than any creature on Pax did."

Insulted, Sigil's head swung toward the irritation snacking at her side. "I cared for him on Pax."

Meeting her eyes, Sovereign conceded. "You did. And he will see to you here in return."

She knew what he was about. "Jerla is only a child. It is wrong for you to use him in such a way."

The man shook his head, his dark hair shifting like the waves outside. "You killed his mother. You exterminated every last lifeform on Pax. He's all that's left."

She thinned her lips to stop them from trembling. "I didn't mean to."

There was a trace of pity reflected in the hardness of his expression. "I know."

He held up what remained of the fruit in offering.

Sigil took a slimy sliver, chewed and swallowed, tasting nothing. "I know what you're doing."

Any creature who has survived torture understood the stage where their assailant built rapport. Sovereign nodded. "I know."

"Are you going to rape me now?"

Those eyes, those deep, strange eyes looked unbelievably sad. "You were not cured of your compulsion. Such a thing was ingrained into your very thinking and chemical response to various stimuli. Do you want to be left feral in a cage with no future? Or do you want freedom and life?"

She let him see how weak she'd become. "I want to go home..."

"Que is dead. You have no home."

Chapter 2

Apart from waking that first morning in her strange rooms, Sigil was never left alone. Sovereign was always with her. He even slept at her side—as if certain she would not reach over in the dark and rip out his throat. He held her when she would not move, and spoke softly of things she paid no attention to. The sound of his voice became as common as the sound of waves breaking outside the open balcony doors, ambient music Sigil subconsciously paced her breath to.

Sorrow physically numbed, but the cost of expanding her chest, of drawing in air—each inhale seared beyond her grief. The sensation was welcome. The pain was deserved, such a fate earned for failing her only friend... for losing her home.

Whatever Sovereign had planned for her, whatever horrors waited, Sigil no longer cared.

He turned her body, rolling her away from the place where glassy eyes stared out toward the sky, and tucked her under his chin.

Blood returned to a leg that had grown sensationless, the man rubbing at Sigil's hip as if he felt her subsequent prickly discomfort.

"It's time to get out of bed."

Getting out of bed usually entailed Sovereign carrying her to some other quadrant of her dwelling's four rooms and four seasons. She slept in Summer where the sun set the room alight at dawn. Food was served in fragrant Spring, something always waiting atop the long table no matter the hour. Bathing took place in Winter, in a large heated pool surrounded by dripping mosaic walls cut from ice. In Autumn waited a sitting room, full of objects, hand selected to amuse her: ancient books with leather bindings—as rare and valuable as the bible Sovereign had offered her on Pax—puzzles strewn about, an alcove filled with fire, surrounded by black marble almost as imposing at the man who laid her on the nearby divan.

No tech existed beyond outdated lighting systems that did little more than glow. No access panels, no holographic entertainment relays. The nearest thing to scientific achievement was a large winding clock built into the Autumn room's massive window. As the hours dragged by, the huge hands moved, changing the shadows of the room to mimic leaves falling from a tree.

Secluded with the Irdesian Emperor, his Brothers would seep into other seasons—leaving food, laying out the simple attire Sovereign would pull over her head after they were finished in the bathing pool. She sensed their proximity, yet never saw a one.

Karhl, his psyche familiar to her, would approach the nearest. Yet he never fully intruded.

He just wanted her to know he was there.

The emotions she sensed from the lurking Lord Commander were always steady, always reassuring. In fact, there were no minds anywhere near her that were not absolutely composed.

No matter which room she was placed in, sleep consumed most of her hours. In Winter's heated pool she would doze against Sovereign's chest as he bathed her, the food in Spring swallowed by a sleepy, disinterested woman.

And in Autumn, stretched out on the soft divan, cradled, she could blank out amidst the scents of leather and flame. Or it may have been the habit of the male who sat at the end of the cushions. The one who held her feet on his lap, rubbing them lazily, which made slumber easy.

Zombie-like, she put up no resistance, and made no effort to flee what she had termed her 'due punishment'.

What would be the point? Where would she go? There was nothing but an empty universe outside those rooms, a big vast space of loneliness and inevitable suffering. She deserved to be trapped with the enemy. She deserved whatever they had in store for her.

Sigil did not even respond when perfunctory sex was 'applied'.

With each mating, Sovereign did little to seduce beyond assuring her comfort before he filled her with the liquid that maintained sanity. When it was finished, he always kneeled between her spread thighs, their bodies still deeply joined, and would trace a kneading grip over her every muscle. That was where he took his time, unwinding all that unaddressed tension that made Sigil's shoulders stoop.

She wished he wouldn't.

The common occurrence of sex she could abide. Even in grief, Sigil grasped the purpose of living day-to-day outside the omnipresent worry utter madness might consume her at any moment. All the better to feel the pain of her loss; coherency was the perfect punishment. She would even spread willingly when Sovereign lifted her robe, lying still to assure every moment of her sorrow was purely felt.

The communion was so cursory it seemed an endurable chore, and that was what made the ensuing touches so unwelcome. The Emperor paid attention to every part of her flesh while she remained spread, full of him, and limp. He rubbed from fingertips to toes, paid meticulous attention, all the while cooing nonsense she ignored.

Half the time she fell asleep… but that was the thing about time: it wore on. It changed perception, until Sigil began to feel what Sovereign was doing.

The sun was setting the day she took the trouble of moving her eyes. She actually looked at him, as if to ask why he'd even bothered trying to offer comfort. Sovereign had held her gaze, smiling as if to tempt his captive to voice such thoughts, and continued kneading her forearm. She said nothing, simply watched. When Sovereign's strokes neared where he'd just filled her with seed, where he still remained embedded in her quim, as if to test the waters, his thumb pressed her flaccid clit.

Holding her eyes, measured featherlight pressure coaxed Sigil's little nub to harden.

A playful pinch and he whispered, "You're allowed to feel pleasure. I long to give it to you, but I won't force it."

Flicking her bud faster, seeing a twitch in the woman's hips, her little quiver squeezed his cock. He didn't offer more, no firm grip on her breast, no grind of his groin against her, just that maddening, perfect friction rubbing tight circles over rapt nerve endings. Every opportunity was offered for Sigil to slap his hand away. Instead, her breath changed, and a broken grunt caught in her throat.

The wave of accompanying wetness bathed his dick, Sovereign already lying atop her to praise and soothe her orgasm.

"Precious, beloved."

She whimpered, hiccupping and pathetic. Drawing out more, Sovereign pressed kiss after kiss over damp cheeks, riding on the waves of the first emotion his Sigil had shared since the day she woke after so many decades asleep. Reaching between their bodies, his fingers danced as they always did to prepare her. She was still wet, seeping out his ejaculate and the remnants of her orgasm from her squirming. Toying where his shaft invaded, taking time to trace the more delicate stretch of her lips, he felt her leg spread wider. At first invitation, his throbbing cock pistoned hard enough to jar her.

Sovereign moaned, low and grainy, to feel a response, any response.

There was no tender rocking, no sedate caution. Teeth over her jugular, he violated that small tight place with ragged pounding. Jack hammering, soaring to hear Sigil's every breath coated in a cry, he drew her higher. A swirled nipple was sucked into his mouth, a lick between her bouncing breasts, a taste of her parted lips, and a warning.

"You will come again. You will come for me!"

It hurt beautifully.

Or was that pleasure?

Her hips were jerking, Sigil's body exacting in its reaction to being fucked after so many eons of sedate friction. Lips at Sovereign's ear, feeling each violent thrust as he brought her to his lap and held her spread wide, Sigil did what he loved most. She begged, "Please."

Violence broke out—inhuman speed that would have damaged any Convert female beyond repair—Sovereign had her bowed over his arms. Familiar with her brand of pleasure, he collared her throat in one tight hand, so she might see stars as her walls crumbled and her body was taken beyond any sensation another might attempt to give her.

Head thrown back, her nails hooked Sovereign's shoulders as hips ground in time with jarring thrusts. Bouncing on a thick cock, feeling more than superficial gratification, sick with life and death and the continuation of breath when nothing else mattered, she fractured.

Her hair was tugged aside, the man snaking his head far enough around her form to lock his teeth on her nape and bite with vigor. The jolt rocked Sigil the instant vertebrae parted. With her clit throbbing, a twist of muscle strained to tighten and keep each inch of Sovereign's cock in her body—to pull it deeper, to fill the void.

Hearing her choked gasps, Sovereign sprayed against her vacant womb, shooting his mark as deep inside her jerking body as he could. And Sigil, the moment she felt the initial wave of come erupting from the base of such a demanding organ, tightened her legs about his waist.

He gnawed further at her nape, roaring something awful as he lapped at the pinch of skin between his teeth.

When he unhinged his jaw, loosened his stranglehold on her throat, when the female's first deep breath ended her quaking orgasm, Sigil did not weep. Instead, she looked at him as if she did not know he'd even been in the room.

Brushing back hair from her damp forehead, Sovereign grinned wickedly, enjoying that last flickering suck of her cunt milking everything it could get.

"Beloved, you've made me proud. You are very brave."

Why had he called her brave? What was brave in surrender?

After laying her down, Sovereign slept as he always did, holding her, their legs entwined. But that night, Sigil found no peace in sleep's oblivion.

Looking at the line of him in the dark, seeing with eyes designed to adjust to low light, Sigil found no answer in Sovereign's musculature, his inky waved hair, or the angles of his face. Scooting back, attempting to disengage from his touch, what she found instead was Sovereign's eyes flaring open.

He watched her every move, but he said nothing.

The increase in her heart rate was abnormal. Confusion followed. After several uneven breaths, Sigil turned away. He closed the space. Solid, muscular chest pressed to her back, Sovereign's arms once again tightened around her.

The sound of surf, the constant breeze, and the soft breaths of the man once again in sleep… Sigil finally had an opinion about them. They were too loud, too real, distracting from where her mind should be wallowing in the memory of Que.

Lying there through the subsequent hours went from tedious to uncomfortable. She was hungry, aching, forlorn, and lost when the beast at her back finally stirred. The instant he tried to lift her so they might bathe, she moved out of his reach.

"Hush, beloved." He had her wrist in his grip before Sigil could evade completely. "There is no need to panic. You're safe here."

Safe from what?

Tired eyes looked to where he dared to restrain her, and Sigil found her arm had grown thin.

As if reading her thoughts, Sovereign explained, "You're weak because you hardly eat."

Voice rough from disuse, Sigil grunted. "Let go."

He did, Sigil slipping awkwardly from her odd crouch on the bed.

Sovereign smiled at her. "You look tired. Have you slept?"

"No." Why had she answered him? Why did her voice sound gritty and foreign?

Dark brows rose, the bastard finding her reply curious. "And you're hungry?"

Even with his hands offering succor, even with calm emotions projected, she was wary of him. Every word Sovereign had ever spoken in her presence carried the weight of extreme intention. He was molding a response, guiding, breaking—a force Sigil found intimidating and equally disturbing. Especially as Sovereign was internally triumphant beyond his handsome, carefully organized expression.

Had Que seen her at that moment, backing away—not from Sovereign, but from whatever was hurtling around inside her when she looked at him— he would have been disappointed.

Only the weak refused to face their flaws.

Sovereign was her flaws personified.

Watching as he cautiously approached, Sigil tried to articulate her thoughts. All that passed her lips was one long breath of, "Que is dead. I saw his head in a box."

Already in Sovereign's embrace, crushed so she might have something to fight besides herself, he sighed. "Let me help you, Sigil."

Hands that had become familiar went right to her nape and rubbed hard enough involuntary muscle relaxation almost made her sag to the ground.

Moving a fat tongue, forcing more from a throat that gave only croaky, hoarse grunts, Sigil accused, "You bit me."

Warm lips pressed to her hairline, Sovereign smiled. "Not hard. And you came beautifully as I did. It is time now for you to make peace with what you are, reconcile your regrets, and embrace this new life. In the five months since you woke, have I given you one reason to fear? Have I hurt you? You know you are safe with me."

Five months? That wasn't possible.

"You told me you wouldn't bite me... you lied."

Sovereign's expression made it clear he felt no guilt for closing his teeth on her neck. "Long ago, under different circumstances, I did. But if that's what it took to wake you up, then I would break that oath a thousand times over. Should you wish to punish me for it, grow stronger. As of now, you stand no chance of victory on any scale."

The Emperor could not be more right.

He pulled her to Winter. While they bathed, Sigil wouldn't let him touch her, hissing if Sovereign tried to help, and absolutely refusing to let him comb out her hair.

After dressing quickly, with the day's gown hanging from one shoulder and stuck to damp skin, Sigil left him to find food in Spring.

Much more than food awaited her.

Karhl stood from the table's head seat the instant she paced through the archway. Two work roughened palms took her face, fingers lacing into dripping silvery hair, and a warm mouth crashed down to claim hers. The urgency of his unanticipated attention, the forthright possession, made Sigil squeak.

Karhl was relentless. If a man could hold centuries of longing for a woman and pour it into one kiss, that was surely what he bestowed on her.

And then it was over, both of them breathing hard. Realizing she stood stiff like a lightning struck tree, Sigil lowered tense arms from where they hovered stiff at her sides, and felt Sovereign's consciousness enter the room behind her.

Karhl seemed unmoved that a third had joined their private moment, too busy studying her face, tracing her swollen lower lip with one large thumb. "I have missed you." He still spoke with little expression, hiding far more jubilant emotions behind the quasi-Axirlan mask.

At her back was the heat of another body, then the quick, sure tugs of a comb through wet hair.

"Sigil was eager to find you. She ran straight out of the bath."

A fire roared in sea glass eyes, and Karhl looked down at his female, found pert nipples showing dark pink through wet fabric, and offered a filthy groan. "Have her boy fetch her something dry."

Boy? Jerla…

"No." Sigil walked away from both the one untangling the last bit of her hair and from the giant pleased to his core to see her, taking the seat at the head of the table.

She began to eat.

Fingers in her mouth, grabbing at whatever was nearest, she chewed and swallowed, careless of what had been expertly prepared, displayed, and offered. Karhl sat at her left, Sovereign at her right, the males partaking of the meal with far more grace than the starving female.

They began to speak with one another openly of government business. On occasion, one of them would offer her a dish out of her dirty-fingered reach, or they would open the rind of a complicated fruit, crack a shellfish, refill her glass, as if such an exchange were natural.

Sigil ate until her stomach ached, looking over the destruction she'd wrought upon the table as Karhl mixed some beverage with warm water, to set it before her.

"Ango will ease your stomach."

If she was lucky, it might be poison. Wishing so, she met his eyes and swallowed the small offering in one gulp. The ache in her belly subsided. Sigil frowned.

The men went back to talking, perhaps even talking to her, but Sigil's attention was caught on a foreign sound beyond breaking waves and male voices. Laughter, giddy and fresh—a child's noise—came from Autumn.

Standing, she left them to iron out policy, politics, war effort— whatever— and crossed the circular anteroom. Leaning against Autumn's arched entry, Sigil watched Jerla explore her untouched gifts. A master of self-entertainment, the Tessan boy found everything wonderful, and had no shame in piling up the best by his estimation, to spread out and play with.

There was so much life in that yellow swishing tail, an eagerness to exist. Fascinated, afraid to interrupt his games, Sigil waited as silent as a killer in the dark. Jerla did not notice her for quite some time, and had the stack of treasures he was making not tumbled, he may never have.

Sigil was far more startled than him, her hand gripping the archway like a shield before her body.

Eyes, shining in their black totality, caught her, the boy instantly silent.

Recognizing the awkwardness of hiding herself from a child, Sigil straightened and said, "There is food in Spring, if you hunger."

Talons hovering over a toppled music box, Jerla shook his head. Considering her, reptilian in the angle of his neck, the child blurted, "Lord Commander Karhl shared while you were in the bath."

"What did you like best?"

Picking up the cause of distorted music, Jerla crooned, "The Turlanqi mousse."

Which one had that been? Her Tessan boy had grown since she'd last seen him.

Wiping her dirty fingers on the side of her drying gown, Sigil stepped nearer. "Are you happy here?"

Straightening from his pile of sparkling items, Jerla reached for something new and padded over ruby carpet to offer it. An etched board decorated by his talons and painted to show Pax was given with timid enthusiasm. "I made this for you."

Sigil, seeing their old home through the eyes of a child, found great worth in the artistry. Jerla had not intended it, she was sure, but there was nothing beautiful in Pax's shape. It seemed fitting. Pax had never been beautiful, but crusted and festering. The only beautiful thing on that board was the intention behind the artwork.

"Do you miss your mother, child?"

She'd upset him, Sigil could sense the disrupted feelings of a boy who bravely kept his expression closed. Trying to smooth it over, she amended, "I have been told you are cared for now. I wanted that for you."

"Imperial Consort, don't make me leave."

"Why would I do that?"

"You want to send me away. You want me to go to the sands. But I want to stay with you."

Looking at the shy boy, Sigil demanded, "Did someone tell you to say that?"

Artfully, Jerla did not answer the question. Instead he shared his own desire for the future, "We could have adventures."

He had either been well coached or truly meant what he said. It was impossible to sense the outright motivation in a mind so young and simple. Stepping closer, Sigil took the music-box from his hands, looking at the ornate device.

A voice came from behind her. "That was a gift from the wife of Magister Belloy, her name is Delphine. Formerly of House Kator."

Magister was a high rank amongst the Brotherhood. It gave the bearer control over a planet, sometimes even whole systems, if Sigil remembered correctly. Looking at the frivolous box, she cracked the lid. There was a small plaque inside:

I have longed to meet you.

"Human treachery?"

"No." There was a smile, amusement, in Sovereign's voice as he stepped nearer. "Matron Delphine is a human of merit, well-loved by your Brother. Belloy honors her so highly he petitioned the throne to allow his wife the honor of bearing offspring that would take his name."

Staring at where Jerla had gone back to playing, where the child ignored them in place of a glowing disk of some strange mineral, Sigil frowned. "If you can breed with humans, then why am I here?"

A light stroke on her cheek and Sovereign whispered, "We can't. And who he chose to sire his children is a private understanding between Belloy and his wife."

"But *you* know…" He'd have to in order to maintain total control. "More importantly, does she know they are not his?"

Sovereign only smirked, eyes alight, and assured, "And you are here because I adore you." Wiping where food crumbled from her skirt, he continued, "Even smeared with breakfast."

"I'm here," Sigil sighed, walking deeper into the room, "because I deserve to be here."

"Exactly." The man turned to face her, eyes fervent as he took her limp hand. "You deserve to be here, beloved. You'll understand that in time."

First Karhl had poured oceans of feeling over her, sealed in a kiss. Now, Sovereign was doing the same, stroking damp hair from her face.

She deserved torment, not monsters pretending to be lambs. Turning to view the Tessan boy, Sigil asked, "Does Jerla know I killed his mother?"

The child's eyes darted up, full of heartbreak.

"It was an accident, but it was my fault. Did you know that, boy? Did they tell you that you are here to amuse the creature who murdered your only family?"

The boy fled the room in such a state, Sovereign hissed. "Was that necessary? You feel it is acceptable to torment a child in such a way?"

Glacial eyes flashed back to the man thinking to correct her. "He wanted to join me on adventures. You've poisoned his mind into loving me!"

"Sigil, consider what you've just done. You were his hero, something to hold onto, and you took that away out of spite. Do not lie to me, or yourself, by claiming disclosure was better for him, that it will improve his life in any way. You robbed that child. Could you not be the figurehead of his admiration? Could you not have let him be happy?"

Sovereign's attempt to compound her guilt earned her anger. She spoke the truth. "I am dangerous. Jerla should never have been allowed anywhere near me. And he certainly should not have been coaxed to admire me!"

The man's frustration was palpable. "You are all he has left, no matter the oddity of your tie. Learn to curb your impulses and forget the castigation the dead Axirlan forced you to swallow. There is nothing wrong with what you are."

Yanking from his grip, Sigil slunk away, furious to hear Que spoken of as a tyrant. "And what would you have me do for the boy? Bounce him on my knee? Make a replacement companion for him?"

Sovereign let her have her space, releasing a thick breath. "Arden is to be your companion, Karhl your guardian. They will help you navigate society and your position in it. Jerla will be whatever you wish for him to be, but cruelty does not suit you, Sigil."

Heavier guilt began to overshadow her grief. "I killed his mother. I slaughtered everyone on Pax. And it wasn't the first time I was responsible for such a horror."

"Drinta killed them by attempting to wield a weapon far beyond her control. Furthermore, your psionics have been repaired—a frenzied burst of that magnitude is not something you need to fear anymore. And I know you fear yourself. That is why you have made no attempt to test your new limits. It is time to grow past juvenile denial of your new situation and embrace your role here."

Why did she feel this whole thing had been staged, as if she had been played by an expert? "You knew what I would say to Jerla. You knew he shouldn't be exposed to me."

Sincerity was all too keen in Sovereign's emotions. "I hoped for better."

"Who is going to comfort the boy?"

"Arden is close with your Jerla." Sovereign shifted his face into expressionlessness. "He will tend him well enough."

The Herald who'd haunted her through Pax possessed a silver tongue—he would say exactly the right thing to bring Jerla back into loving a woman he should hate. Confused by why that thought offered equal parts comfort and regret, Sigil sighed and went to pick up the child's abandoned mess.

Putting the objects back where Jerla had found them, she tried to ignore how closely Sovereign was watching her—as if her actions betrayed something she couldn't quite touch on.

She stopped at an inlaid game board, toying with the pawns, wondering if Jerla could teach her how to play the game. That was a good way to win a child's favor, wasn't it?

So much light played off the game piece pinched between her fingers, such a shine it seemed keen to dazzle and manipulate her attention, just as she considered manipulating Jerla. A fist formed around the little figure, so tight Sigil's fingers ached. Furious at what she'd done, a gathering blue psionic charge distorted the air around her hand. On a whim, she threw the board, dashing the pieces against the wall with little more than a thought.

And then it was over. No more excruciating bursts of energy came on the heels of her anger, no wild abandon to tear the room apart.

A wash of strange heat moved over the side of her skull.

No blood dripped from her nose.

It was as Sovereign said… she'd been repaired, muted, weakened.

Dropping the token from her grip, glacial eyes moved toward the spectator, and Sigil snarled lowly, "I hate you."

Every word was true. Sigil hated him almost as much as she hated herself.

Chapter 3

"I hate you."

Watching Sigil stand so still, her face alive with regret, Sovereign disagreed. "You don't mean that."

Oh, she meant it. Even he could see that she felt it so thoroughly that her lower lip trembled. That brand of hatred had begun in the cradle, had been the flavor of her childhood, and the bane of all her years free of Condor.

Cut from stone, grim, Sovereign warned her. "My love has always been yours, and though yours should have been mine, I am left with your *hate* instead. And it still changes nothing in my regard, or the difficulty of my position, precious Sigil."

She gave him her back, earning an unseen sneer from the male.

Sovereign openly prowled, caging her in. "And you think I take pleasure in forcing you? That I have enjoyed these last months watching you lie like a penitent accepting the whip? All so I might attend an unresponsive body in an effort to heal you? This monster you have labeled me out of your stubbornness and abstention bears no resemblance to the man I am! There is no length I would not go to for you. No limit, Sigil!"

Forcibly turning her, gripping a stuttering chin, Sovereign made her look. "I understood your sorrow; I know the exact pain you carry, and since you woke, never once did I force pleasure in an effort to steal your attention before you were ready to give it. No matter what revulsion you bear for me, even you cannot question my *faithfulness,* my *sacrifices,* or my *patience*."

It was her whimper that stopped Sovereign from closing his mouth over hers to suck in a kiss that would have been rough and selfish.

Setting her free, edging back, he let his expression mirror the determination inside him. "I will break you of this ingrained response and you will love me. It is inevitable."

Showing teeth, Sigil hissed. "It wouldn't be real."

The nearest bauble went shattering against the wall as he raged. "Your hate is what is not real! And you dared to call your Brothers the sheep. At the honest heart of it, Sigil, you do not even try to think past your programing. You only run from it. You *hate* me because your handlers were very thorough in planting that idea, in torturing you into mental submission. Take a hard look at yourself and tell me that is not true."

Voice rising, Sigil demanded, "And why should I?"

A look of smug superiority made beautiful lips mean. "Where is your self-righteousness now, madam hypocrite? I thought you believed you were above us all, so determined in your liberated sense of self. Yet here you are, still that little girl on Condor."

He'd talked her into a circle. To contradict him would make her look foolish. To agree would be an obvious falsehood. There was too much truth in his claim. Her hatred of him was ingrained so deeply, the thought of even trying to align his image with fondness would naturally never occur to her.

Sovereign was borderline mocking, twirling a length of her hair about his finger. "Are you afraid to think for yourself? You are floundering already. To lose your programed foundation must seem terrifying indeed."

She was many things, but she was not a coward. Even on Condor, even young and vulnerable, she'd faced every last goddamn thing her handlers had laid out for her. Furious, her fist smashed into his jaw. The force had rocked Sovereign's head to the side, but he did nothing more than swing his gaze back to her in response. "That's right. That is what you were trained for, that's why Commander Dimitri made you."

The burn of his words drained away her fleeting exultation. Staring at him for a long moment, blinking oddly, Sigil took a step back.

Her whisper took a great deal of effort. "That is what I was trained for…" Memories older than her time with Que rushed in so hard they began to blend together. Combat practice, poisons, murder, friendlessness, sociopathy, viciousness, pain. "I learned how to kill you a thousand different ways."

Dulcet coolness enriched Sovereign's voice. "And when I lay dead how would you feel?"

Free?

He answered her silence. "You would be lonely, beloved, even more so than you already are. Deep down, under all your broken pieces, the truth is that I have been your constant companion—a whisper in your mind from the very beginning."

Eyes closed, it was almost like he wasn't really there, and for a movement Sigil felt she might will him away. But then he touched his lips to hers, and where every part of her longed to lash out, she stilled to prove that she could bear it on his terms.

She could kiss him without the effect of passion having forced it. She could offer an attempt.

It was the response he wanted, and knowing he was pleased only stirred up more vitriol in her being. When it was done, when she had returned the pressure of a chaste kiss, he smiled, happy.

"You can't attribute all my hatred to Condor." The man before her was not a saint. There were things he'd done—things he'd claimed he'd done for her—that Sigil found disturbing to an extreme. And had he never come to Pax, Que would still be alive.

For that he had to pay.

With hesitant fingers Sigil reached up to touch his face, her eyes wet. She'd promised him punishment if he didn't kill her when they first faced off in her lost home. He would receive it.

Tracing the precision of his bone structure, she had to admit Sovereign was beautiful, perfect. And while he looked at her in love, she took what was hers.

Ripping his left eye from his skull was simple.

Dangling the little globe by its blood vessels and torn nerve above parted lips, Sigil dropped it, swallowing that pretty eye whole, facing him unashamed as it slithered down into her belly.

Sovereign stood, pressing the flat of his palm to the gaping, bloody eye socket. His lack of retaliation confused her automatic response. There was no anticipated battle, just awkward silence and a rolling sense of burdened grief.

Inside and out the Emperor was in pain, but it hardly showed beyond the tightening of his brow and the thinning of his lips.

Tired, Sigil walked out of the room.

In Summer she'd slept, too exhausted for even the midday sun blazing off the walls to wake her.

When a rumbling stomach finally drew her back to life, two moons rose over the night-darkened sea outside her balcony. There was silence and no trace of Sovereign's mind. But she had not been abandoned.

Karhl waited for her, and the nearby course of his emotions was strong.

Padding barefoot over cool floors, Sigil sought out what was her due—having faced enough punishment in her life to know when her judge sat waiting to dole it out.

Dried rusty splashes of gore still stained her fingertips, her dress was still mussed from breakfast. Pale and resigned, she walked straight-backed through the archway of Spring.

The Lord Commander stood as if part of the architecture. Lacking the armor he'd worn in the early hours, he posed. A black uniform, much like the one Sovereign wore day after day, stretched across his mass. It did nothing to soften his severity.

It seemed he had also brought witnesses. A collection of Sovereign's Brothers—five members of Project Cataclysm—sat at the long table, just as noiseless as the Lord Commander.

Before they could begin, Sigil stated, "I regret nothing."

Karhl moved his head just enough for the metal discs in his hair to chime. "Not even what you said to Jerla?"

Rubbing her lips together Sigil looked away. That she did regret…

The low base of his voice stated the obvious. "You anticipate punishment for your earlier behavior." Karhl made no effort to approach nearer when she toed a step, as if to brace and physically defend herself. "I expected you to be timid. I did not expect you to be frightened, young one." As usual there was no emotion shown in his expression, the comfort he crooned at her came from within. "This is not Condor. No Brother gathered here would dare touch you without your express permission.”

No matter how tranquilly Karhl projected his emotion, Sigil refused to lower her guard and believe him. “Sovereign wishes to punish me himself?”

“I know my Brother. More than anything, Sovereign would wish to be the one to soothe your worries. But his presence is not best for you at this moment.” Three steps and Karhl pulled out her chair so Sigil might be tempted to sit.

Eyeing him with suspicion, she slithered into it, tense.

Ignoring how she braced for a blow, the Lord Commander introduced each Brother sitting around her table. A Herald of the Second Sphere, Mathias, smiled, teeth white against dark skin. To his left sat two of six Imperial Admirals. Parnisu, the taller, explained that he’d controlled the ship that had pulled her out of Pax, and seemed to study her even more closely than she studied him. Gethman, sable hair straight as a pin, mirrored his compatriot’s uniform, but seemed more at ease, lounging back in his chair like a spoiled cat.

No rank was given to the two remaining men. From the symbols woven into the drape that hung from their shoulders, Sigil was certain the pair were *High Adherents*—something Converts considered holy men. It was their Order that managed galactic conversion, human laws, and execution of the *Unsalvageable*. Dryden offered a nod, his expression soft and made to be beautiful. Corths, upturned eyes so very Tessan, dared much, reaching out as if he thought to stroke her cheek.

She jerked her head away.

Apologetic in tone, Corths explained. "Sweet Sister, I am the one who watched over your keeping, day and night, as you slept."

Jade eyes looked at her as if they were familiar, and in Corths's estimation, they were. Even though he'd failed to touch her, Sigil felt the ghost sensation of a repetitive stroke over her face—a memory in mirror to where he must have pet her often in her sleep.

Sigil turned her gaze away from him, just as she would dissuade any spectator overexcited by her performance at Swelter.

The Lord Commander began to spoon food onto her plate.

Not one of them seemed troubled by her reticence, serving themselves and conversing as if she had not ingested their leader's eye only hours earlier. Instead, they asked gentle questions she didn't answer, behaving as if she were one of them come home. But worse was the constant distraction, the obviousness that Sovereign was not in attendance.

Her eyes were drawn to search the corners for him, and it bothered her that another sat in his chair.

The wound she'd given him was not fatal, minor even in the scheme of things. It would take a few days for his eye to regenerate, but the dinner seemed to suggest he would not return until healed.

Liberation from his presence felt abnormal, uncomfortable even, and then it struck her why Karhl was overly cautious, why so many Brothers had been collected.

Sovereign was not going to be the one to *tend to her compulsion…*

She spoke at last. "He's not coming back tonight. I have been handed off so I might learn my place."

A large hand covered hers. Dwarfing her fingers. Karhl spoke softly. "It is your nature to see plots where there are none. Such apprehension was necessary to prior survival, but it complicates this stage of grief. You're angry, regretful, and bound to lash out. I understand. Sovereign understands. So you must not judge him too harshly for retreat when your behavior has disappointed his overzealous hopes. I know it is difficult for him to finally hold you, only to gain cruelty and suspicion in return."

Lips in a line, she glared at the white-haired warrior.

Karhl leaned nearer, looming so she might pay attention. "Imagine seeing the thing you want most suffer, even under your best care. Imagine your Que looking at you with hatred, no matter how delicate you are in seeing to his needs. Now, imagine after decades of service a few precious moments of recognition from the one you love crashing apart before they could be truly relished."

Why would he dare to say that name? Gritting her teeth, Sigil spat, uncaring who their audience was. "Sovereign is not Que!"

"No." Karhl agreed. "You are Sovereign's Que, you always have been. And just like your Que could never love you, you have never loved him. It is a tragedy he bears with dignity."

Why the fuck should she care? That man deserved what she'd done to him. "He should never have let Jerla in here!"

"Jerla has begged to see you every day since he first laid eyes on you. I know what you said to the child. I understand the part of you that felt that you needed to say it. But I must remind you that unlike the Axirlans I mimic in appearance and you strain to mimic in thinking, we are not of that species. Axirlan creed is limited by their inability to feel, and no matter how magnificent you find the concept, you are not Axirlan. Blatant honesty is not always best to curb remorse. You have a duty to that boy."

Her mouth moved before her brain could stop her. "Is that why Arden is not here? Jerla is still very upset?"

It seemed for a moment Karhl would not answer. His face and demeanor unchanging, the Lord Commander finally asked, "Do you desire his company?"

Which *he* Karhl referred to was left vague. Either way the answer was simple. "No."

Karhl had more to say. "Are you unhappy that tonight I will attend you? You wish Sovereign would return?"

The tactile oddity of separation from Sovereign's presence was a clear sign he was having some deeper effect on her. Separation would clear her mind. "I do not."

No hesitation came with the justification of what Karhl wanted. "Then you understand that regression is likely and will need to be seen to." A male who had never shown intonation let his voice grow husky, Karhl's vivid eyes moving to her mouth. "But, beautiful young one, I long greatly to take you willingly to bed, and would hate to force you should you slip and grow dangerous to yourself."

"My psionics have been repaired. How dangerous could I be?"

An infinitesimal smile came to the corners of Karhl's mouth. "I think you have proven this morning just how dangerous you can be."

Cocking a brow, Sigil grew brazen. "I warned him on Pax that if he didn't kill me, I would make him pay for all the years he's hounded me. You were there, you heard my words. He's lucky I only took one eye."

Sigil was not sure if it was due to his Axirlan nature or the presence of the other Brothers, but Karhl's vast internal amusement didn't show. Remaining deadpan, he agreed. "You are a woman of your word, which is why I asked our Brothers to join us for dinner and act as my protection."

God help her, but she chuckled before she could stop herself. In response, he gripped the seat of her chair and scooted Sigil nearer. "Your Brothers have come to cheer you, and should you encourage it, some may wish to watch our mating, others to enhance it. But that is entirely up to you."

Ignoring how Karhl's great hand began to stroke her thigh, Sigil grew blunt. "And if I don't want to fuck you or serve as the night's entertainment?"

"Then you won't." Steady, the Lord Commander removed his hand and offered her a modicum of space. "You are not a pleasure slave and I meant every word. No Brother here will touch you, and I would only move against your wishes if I had to. Should you not accept me, that time *will* come—maybe not tonight—but I will have to overcome your compulsion should you become dangerous to yourself."

The man's statement confused her just enough for Sigil to say, "So you are not going to force me now? Sovereign would not have waited."

Karhl countered in favor of his Brother. "Sovereign had no choice when you refused to communicate and were difficult to read. You needed structure and a schedule. My actions would have been no different. Everything he did was done to keep you as comfortable as possible."

Hums of approval and outright agreement came from the collected Brothers.

It all felt like some great test. Some invisible carrot dangled before her face, a secret prize that was waiting—all she had to do was engage in sex with the large white-haired warrior whose emotions sang to her even though he eyed her with placid curiosity.

She had her own test for them. "If you say I can choose, then I choose not to."

Nodding that he understood, Karhl agreed. "As you wish."

"And now that it's settled," Parnisu, still unsmiling, interjected, "perhaps you will relax and allow us the honor of getting to know you."

They wanted her to speak. Fine.

The meal was lengthy, Sigil easing into the strangeness of sitting with so many survivors of Project Cataclysm. Remembering to eat was sometimes tricky when she was too busy calculating escape routes, or deciding whose neck she would have to break first if they were to attack her.

Not a one made advances, they only wanted to know simplicities: her opinion on climate, food preferences, what colors she favored. Mildly intrusive questions into her history followed, focused on time periods the Brotherhood had evidently collected detailed intelligence on. Had she enjoyed the society of Desvop Outreaches? Did she favor Tessans or Sudenovans? How is it that she had never been to any Axirlan cities? What did she think of feral humans? Was it true she hated Converts?

During questioning, her Brothers held various offerings forward, the men behaving as if eager for her to learn the names of dishes. It was a game, Sigil found. To varying degrees they all tried to make physical contact with her—touching her when passing food, trying to feed her with their fingers—as if *they* fed off the exchange. Karhl was the most blatant, moving her hair to run a single stroke down her nape each time strands fell forward to mingle in the gravy on her plate.

Each of the men were so very different, yet exactly alike underneath their beautiful faces and alternate genetic gifts.

They were all one hundred percent committed to their cause.

The meal ended.

On some unseen command, both Dryden and Corths stood. The High Adherents—the ones she looked at with the greatest suspicion—bowed, but wisely kept their distance. Though Corths paused, let his eyes shine with childlike innocence and asked softly, "May I, just once?"

Stiff, Sigil said nothing. The High Adherent took silence as acceptance, running the backs of his fingers down her cheek. The moment was short, and he left the instant his touch receded.

For her behavior, Herald Mathias grinned, teasing, "If I ask for a kiss will I get one?"

Her narrowed eyes, the Herald was wise enough to accept as negation. Chuckling, Mathias winked, stood, and followed his Brothers out.

Parnisu and Gethman remained.

During the meal, they had been the quietest—watching, strategizing. It matched their design, and simplified their place in her estimation: warriors, third rank, who lacked the charisma of a Herald or the pseudo-religious fervor of High Adherents. And there were three more admirals just like them somewhere in the Empire waiting their turn to sit at her table.

Gethman seemed to speak for them both. "I have two male charges under my name, my human wife's sons from her previous marriage. Familiar with youths, I suggest that after you wake and are attended to, your Jerla may enjoy showing you his favorite places outside. Neutral ground will simplify reestablishing your unification."

There was a deeper suggestion under Gethman's advice, because in order to follow it, she had to be *attended to*. The admirals were enticing her to mate with Karhl, giving her an opportunity to assure she was free of her compulsion, and offering what they deemed might be a worthy temptation for her effort.

Looking him dead in the eye, Sigil challenged, "Do you love your convert wife?"

Expanding the tenuous conversation, Gethman said, "To maintain the Imperial hierarchy, most of your Brothers have taken spouses from what had been the strongest human houses or conquered monarchies. As such, we have absorbed them into our influence. We permeate their old and new rivalries, and enforce compliance to authority. The majority are political unions."

A polite way of saying no.

Grinning at her obvious distaste, Gethman ran a hand through his hair and admitted, "I am saddled with a difficult wife. Others are less lucky. Arden, for example, has three from three rival houses." As if sharing something comical, he lifted his glass. "It is fairly common for his ladies to try and assassinate one another."

"How many wives does Sovereign have?"

The admiral hesitated, as if choosing his words carefully. "Your position was designed and honored from the moment the Empire formed. Imperial Consort is above any human concept of wife."

Seeing three warriors seemingly made uncomfortable by a subject so mundane brought the smallest of smirks to her face. "How many concubines?"

"Do you understand what you are?" Parnisu answered for his Brother, still watching her to the point it was unsettling. "Other females cannot threaten your position."

She didn't know why she found it amusing. Perhaps it was the awkward defensiveness buried behind three warrior-still expressions. Or maybe it was the nature of what they all seemed to expect of her. "Other females can have him."

The two admirals did not seem to understand her feelings on the subject, looking to one another in silent communication. Where Gethman was baffled, Parnisu was annoyed, his feelings on the topic made clear when he grunted, "Until your Brothers are given true mates, how long do you really think we would keep him from you?"

What had been a mischievous smirk faded into a sneer.

"Sigil," It was the first time Karhl had spoken since the topic began. "Admiral Parnisu did not mean to offend you."

Cold eyes snapped to the Lord Commander. "And just how many of you are queued up for my theoretical offspring?"

Tangling thick fingers in her hair, Karhl eased nearer. "I desire only you, and no daughter of the Emperor would change that."

That was not what she'd asked. Sigil was aware he knew she was an empath—suspecting he'd altered his phrasing to distract or lie by omission. Far more direct in tone she asked again, "How many of you are there?"

Karhl took a deep breath, studied the way her hair ran through his fingers, and said, "Less than two hundred remain."

It seemed impossible. There was no way an entire species could have been dominated by so few. Trying to find the words led to false starts, but eventually she blurted, "On Condor... I was taught Project Cataclysm's leadership and Special Forces numbered in the high thousands."

"We did." Holding her eyes, Karhl stroked that soft bit of silvery hair between his fingers. "When Condor fell and we openly defended you, the Alliance moved to immediately eradicate us all, expediting our insurgency four years ahead of schedule. Victory required great sacrifice. In the beginning, gaining a foothold in the universe, plowing through human populations, was inelegantly accomplished. The remaining losses were accrued in further campaigns, assassinations… the lower ranks lacked the elites' genetic enhancements and expired from age as humans do. If you wish to know the details, Arden has a written account he prepared while you were sleeping. The volumes are in your Autumn room."

She'd seen the journals shelved near the fire. Once or twice Sovereign had read from them while she'd napped. Looking from the Lord Commander to the one who seemed most aggressive, Sigil asked Admiral Parnisu, "And what if I birthed only boys?"

Resting his elbows atop the table and folding his hands, Parnisu explained. "Sovereign has been altered to suit his purpose as the progenitor of the first true Irdesian house. He can produce only female gametes."

Her captors had always said *daughters*… and she should have known the Brotherhood would have calculated the intended course of their species expansion, strategizing to obtain best results. "And when these daughters are born they will be handed out based on rank…"

Karhl could see the discussion had taken a dangerous turn. "Your children are our children. We would not see them traded as the humans barter their offspring in search of favor or power. They will be worshiped, not subjugated."

Shaking her head, Sigil dislodged her hair from Karhl's fingers and sighed. "And should they choose another path other than the one you will lay out so prettily before them, you will hunt them through the stars and drag them home?"

Gethman smiled and explained the failing in her understanding. "It is natural for a species to seek the comfort of their kind. Some may stray. Most will desire the embrace of family."

"And if you're wrong?"

The smile grew sad. "Then all our kind will die, the human worlds will fall back into chaos, and all our sacrifices would have been for nothing."

Chapter 4

Everything was coated in a soft, spongy moss. And it smelled like… something Sigil could not put her finger on. Running her hands over the ground, she found the sensation calming, friction releasing enough fragrance that she could taste it on her breath. Sun warm on her face, wind teased the strands of hair fallen free from the rope Karhl had woven. The tangles were continually smoothed by the large male keeping her planted with an armored arm around her middle.

Before them, Jerla slept, curled up on the ground with Arden at his side.

The Herald stared openly, smiling to himself as he studied the woman resting pliant against the Lord Commander.

"All is well now. Your little Jerla is content."

Twisting fragments of that strange moss between her fingertips, Sigil glanced up into golden eyes. Unsure if she should comment on the residual sadness infecting the Tessan, she only hummed.

The child had not been expecting her first appearance days ago, oblivious to the amount of high-rank officials congregated when he came out to play on the palace's forested terrace. She sensed his spirits sink at the sight of her. After the first moments of their awkward reunion, after the boy's hesitation and a smiling Arden's assurances, Jerla told her again that he didn't want to go to the sands. The little one swore that he would be good.

It hurt her to hear him so worried he might be cast away. So Sigil behaved exactly as Gethman had suggested—aware the admiral watched keenly from the sideline. Eyeing the wooded space, Sigil found it as detailed—even in its wildness—as her rooms. The garden, if it could be called such, was staged as a primeval forest, made to look as if sprouted from the palace itself. Treetops competed with the roof, vines hung, verdant moss crept up plant life and veiling rocks.

Unsure, Sigil had muttered, "Did you know I can climb higher than anyone here? I can do tricks and I never fall."

The boy, disbelief in his inky-eyed squint, challenged such a statement at once. "You can't do tricks."

"She can," Arden whispered, leaning down to reach the Tessan's unshelled ear. "I've seen it myself. The Imperial Consort can fly."

Karhl's grip on her wrist eased, even he played along with a monotone, "Show him."

Offering Jerla a place on her back, feeling a yellow tail coil tight around her middle, Sigil *took flight*. It may have been some time since her last performance on the silk in Swelter, but her arms knew the dance, and she was supernaturally fast. All the way to the top of the trees she climbed, taking her squealing cargo to peek beyond the foliage.

It was as she assumed, the entirety of the palace was surrounded in ocean, with nothing but endless blue to be seen in all directions.

No wonder they'd let her run free. There was absolutely nowhere to go.

Jerla's arms around her neck tightened, the child mystified. She jumped. He shrieked in delight, and Sigil took him swinging like a monkey through the branches.

Earning the renewed admiration of a child was in parts simple and horrible. Jerla's shining black eyes held wonder, but not as he had before. It was almost as if she were no longer a real thing—as if she'd become something magical and treacherous—an idol Jerla respected and feared.

Easing down in mirror of the sleeping child, Sigil pressed her cheek to the moss. She felt Karhl follow suit to stretch comfortable at her back, and stared at yellow scales. "He'll never love me like he did before."

Arden sighed, though his smile did not falter. "Did you want his love after all? I thought I'd been mistaken in telling him of your wonders, how you'd chosen him—how you'd saved him."

Gentle castigation from Arden seemed odd. It was Sovereign who loved to correct her, Arden who gave her whatever she wanted, and Karhl who strove to make her feel safe. Defensive, Sigil said low enough not to wake the boy, "You think you are very clever, don't you?"

His grin broadened, Arden chuckling softly. "I fall short now and then."

"So which one of you is going to slip into conversation how Jerla's trials parallel those of Converts? That I must be careful what I say to humans?"

Arden outright laughed. "Look who is the clever one."

"Then you will tell me adults are not as resilient or forgiving as children. That I must act like some queen and pretend they don't deserve my pity."

Gold eyes darkened, amusement replaced with a shallow echo of exasperation. "Pity for what? Humanity thrives. Conversion lengthens human lifespans, makes the population resistant to disease, and eager to function as a unit—an inoculation against their inborn inferiority and stimulus to their faulty evolution. We give them purpose. And let's be honest, Sigil. What do you know of humans anyway?"

The Converts she'd come across in the past had only sent her into an uncontrollable rage. She'd killed them, or ran from them if she'd found the willpower to do so. The only Converts she'd seen close up while free of the compulsion were Karhl's altered warriors who guarded her on Pax. They had seemed nothing more than drones lacking personality—cold-blooded and loyal to the cause the universe was wary of inciting.

There was a reason free-humans fled Conversion, refused it, or rebelled.

Sigil could only express her feelings by stating the Irdesian axiom. "Convert or die…"

Shrugging, Arden sprawled and enjoyed the sun. "It is unfair that you judge a people you have never met. Irdesian society would adore you if you would let them, just as Jerla longed to adore you. It is no different, Sigil."

Sleeping beside Karhl greatly reminded Sigil of sleeping beside another. The Lord Commander was warm and bulky, preferring to pull her flush against him, so his bicep might serve as her pillow. The weight of him felt so familiar that sleep came thick.

Sigil had never been much of a dreamer, but flashes haunted her nights in Karhl's weighty embrace—mish-mashed images lacking continuity or purpose. But there was one ongoing theme that slipped in to distract and annoy.

Sovereign.

More than once she'd awoken to see him standing over where she slept confined in Karhl's bulging arms. In the muddled dark, the Emperor would sigh, leaning down to do nothing more than press a kiss to her forehead.

Nightly, he broke her sleep. But when awake, she continued to *feel* his absence, unsure why he watched from the shadows but separated himself from her in the light. Frustrated with the game, Sigil confronted Karhl, demanding an end to the evening visitor.

Standing like a simpleton, Sigil listened as the Lord Commander communicated her vision was impossible.

Sovereign was off-world, far from the Water Palace, sitting the throne on Irdesi Prime.

"Should you wish to go to him, the journey can be arranged."

Somewhat embarrassed, Sigil fussed with her hair so the Lord Commander could not see, and demanded, "Why would I go to him?"

He gave no answer, but sea glass eyes ran briefly over the female body before him, looking a bit longer at the untouched place between her legs. The Lord Commander had kept his word. They'd shared a bed only to sleep, and aside from the thick, nightly reminder of his erection nestled in the cleft of her buttocks, sex was never initiated… at least by Karhl.

She'd been the one to wake with her smiling lips pressed to his neck, her hands all over a body her sleep-drugged mind told her was another's. He'd been Que in scent, in touch, even in his massive pierced organ she dipped into clothing to grip.

For a moment it had been real enough she'd purred, "How I've missed you, Que," only for a great weight to roll her to her back, for Sigil to find herself restrained, recognizing the hardening cock she'd been stroking belonged to another.

Karhl had not taken advantage, he had only stopped her, giving her time to collect herself and fully wake. "Young one, I am not Que."

When her face flamed in shame, he'd said nothing, just tightened his arms in their coil about her body, and rubbed her back leisurely. When they'd gone to bathe, she'd swum the distant length of the warm pool in an effort to create privacy. He had not followed. But when she'd looked to see why, she'd found Karhl's muscled back bowed, the giant bracing one hand against the ice wall. His other hand furiously stroked the very purple cock she'd awakened and refused. On it went until Karhl spurted against the freezing mosaic walls, his face screwed up as if pained.

Sigil had watched what he'd done, her mouth agape, ignoring his clenched buttocks and sculpted musculature in favor of gawking at the scented fluid that ran in thick dribbles down the wall.

Looking over his shoulder, sea-glass eyes found his audience. He turned so she might see him, the ladder of studs that ran down a furiously red cock still clinging to the last dips of come. Her reaction had been almost as strong as if Sigil had felt Sovereign's teeth at her neck. Three sharp pangs made her throb down below, and had she not been submerged, her labia would have been visibly glistening with arousal.

The next day as she bathed, Karhl had done the same: hand bracing against the ice, stroking himself to a groaning eruption she found she could not look away from. And the next, and the next. By the fourth day, she had eased near enough to watch the individual veins pulse in his dick, to know he liked to knead his balls when he ushered forth his ejaculate.

When she approached, Karhl did not spurt on the wall. Instead, he gathered his semen in his cupping hand, watching his female stare riveted as he rumbled, "Come here. It need not be wasted."

Had she not been growing edgier by the day, Sigil might have denied his offer. Instead she climbed from the water. Dripping, she waited, and groaned perversely when he scooped the creamy discharge on two thick fingers to press deep into her pussy. Over and over, Karhl repeated the action, running out of his offering before she could come all over those thick digits.

Her bobbing fingers flicked an aching clit to finish off the exchange, Sigil hardly aware of what she was doing until the ice at her back and the heat hard against her chest registered. She caught herself licking his palm clean, panting and greedy to taste the tang that teased her nostrils each morning.

Karhl could have fucked her right then, and disordered as she was, Sigil would have let him. Instead he cupped her cheek, smiling gently when the female mewled.

Sigil would have sworn he was going to kiss her, her head even tilting back in anticipation. But then nothing, only an exchange of breath, and a single long stroke down her flank. "Jerla is waiting."

What he'd given her, when her body had time to settle from its near frenzy, had lessened the encroaching itch. So much so, the next morning she stood waiting, exercising great willpower to keep her hands at her sides and not fist his magnificent cock until white scented globs might squish out between her fingers. He performed for her, and when Karhl's palm was full, he used his fingers again to deposit his come between her thighs while Sigil squirmed over his hand and crooned.

Overexcited, her pussy clenched around his thick digits and too much semen slipped out to spatter the floor. Seeing what was wasted, knowing she had no right to use him in such a way, Sigil found she'd prefer to *use* another—someone who deserved to serve a purpose and be discarded.

"When is Sovereign scheduled to return?"

Karhl began to pull her toward the pool, continuing with their day as if nothing untoward had transpired. "He will not return, but awaits you at the capital."

Unlike the weather system surrounding the Water Planet where his Sigil was sequestered, gloom encased the Imperial Epicenter. Irdesi Prime was built atop the ruins of the Alliance's Governmental Bastion—a location staked for its defensible perimeter and not its beauty. Due to storms in the upper atmosphere, the twisting sky was in a constant state of flux, offering little visibility from space and muting the light. The dimness turned the city's terraced architecture drab.

Though the capital had been renamed and modernized, it still bore an earthy ugliness. But in the night, that wild sky grew beautiful, the upper atmosphere shimmering with mica as if Irdesi Prime were trapped under fracturing crystal. Like swirling sands, that cloak hid the orange lurking moon from view. But on the rare clear nights, the birthplace of Sovereign, his Brothers, and Sigil could be seen hanging bloated and scarred on the horizon.

Converts considered moon sightings over the capital a bad omen, Adherents' superstition fed to a species easily swayed by crafted religion and tales of the fantastical.

It was almost cause for Sovereign to postpone Sigil's expected arrival. But chances that she even knew that moon was Condor were slim.

Sunlight faded further, the horizon taking on a shock of silver, the brightest fleeting glow Irdesi would feel all day. Rising from the tiered city, a hum began amongst the Converts—a sign of dusk, a programed response every citizen, every pilgrim sung out in collective.

It was meant to be a beautiful moment, ruined when the man at Sovereign's side opened his mouth. "Rumor has spread through the ranks. The long awaited Imperial Consort returns to us at last."

Rumor spread because it was spread by Adherents, the flash in Sovereign's eyes when he looked to his Brother castigating. "Based off a few pleasant meals in her presence, you believe Sigil to be tamer than she is. If you demand too much of her, if you think to put her in front of the masses before she is ready, she will lash out at you."

Dryden was many things, if not optimistic. "Her lamented treatment of Jerla was properly shifted to reflect the Converts' position in her life. The lesson played out perfectly—she is cautious of herself in the child's presence now. Arden even reports the Tessan makes her smile. How much different are humans?"

"You will do as commanded, Brother." There was no question when the Emperor wielded such a tone. "Humans have hurt her, they have hunted her… she will not respond favorably to Convert attention. She hardly responds to attention from her own kind. And you forget, she chose the Tessan child before we found her on Pax. What her reasons were she has yet to fully admit."

There were few in the Brotherhood who would dare question Sovereign's authority, but High Adherents had been chosen because their love to the cause was immaculate. Dryden dared to say, "If she were to know what Converts are, I believe her opinion on the matter would alter drastically."

"Hear me, Dryden." Without taking his attention from the sky, Sovereign addressed the long ago assassin, turned priest, "Sigil is not ready to learn what you propose. In fact, if she were to discover it, I do think she would rampage through your temple, killing the devout first."

The High Adherent clearly did not agree. "You and your secrets, Sovereign. You would keep her ignorant—"

"I would keep her content."

"How cold you are…"

How cold indeed. The very thing he fought to break in Sigil had festered in his own kind—indoctrination. Sovereign shook the severity from his brow, and sighed. "Do not fall into your own dogma. Sigil is not a deity. She's a damaged child who was crafted to hunt us down, one by one, and kill us."

Immediately, Dryden countered. "Her improvement has increased dramatically. The implant functions. Aside from her attack on you, there have been no further incidents. Yet you would keep her under glass and away from her duty to us all."

"You know why I do it!" How Sovereign hated looking from the skyline where Sigil's ship was set to enter dangerous territory to face the *religion* standing at his side. "You dare press a topic in which I have yet to disappoint? Not once have I neglected the Brotherhoods' needs or scorned your expectations. Furthermore, I offered true sacrifice for you all, and in exchange, all High Adherents, *every Brother*, will obey the course I decide is best for her."

The collective had agreed to use force against her. The collective had agreed that physical violation was condoned. Dryden had been the most outspoken. How else was there to be progress that would benefit them all? "When she feels your baby grow inside her,

Sigil will forgive you and understand why it had to be done."

The heart of the issue was so much deeper than the simplicity of stating recent history. "I raped her so none of you would have to. I showed our goddess that she was made of glass, and the divine scorn being ripped from their skies."

Dryden's eyes were a shade of green so catching it was impossible to miss even the slightest movement of his attention. They turned toward Sovereign, the High Adherent daring much to scoff. "Beautifully said. Shall I alter the canon?"

A slow creeping smile grew nasty on Sovereign's beautiful lips. The air about him spiked. If murder had a scent, they both would have breathed the Emperor's intent into every last cell. "Though you are my Brother, my comrade, and my family, I find in this last century that my aversion for High Adherents company grows." They stood toe to toe, Sovereign the clear superior as he crooned the smooth-skulled killer's ancient title. "*Enforcer Second Rank*, do not force me to remind you of your *actual* position... which is not the one dreamed up with ritual, chanting, and prayer."

Serene, seeing a flash over the high grey buildings of the south sector, Dryden smoothed his robes. "My greatest duty is to remind you of yours. That is why you created the Adherents' Order, dear Brother."

A warning look threatened impending doom over the lesser being. Sovereign would only warn him once. "One more fractious word, Dryden, and I will see you set in the tombs. Corths could take your place, and he would not threaten Sigil out of greed or impatience."

Words were offered, hubris replaced with devotion. The man looked sad. "You mistake my motivation. I speak as I do only out of love for her."

Stepping closer, fingers itching to close over an insubordinate throat, Sovereign spoke the truth, "And that *love* which captivates you will only harm her. You do not know Sigil, and your bootlicking devotion will disgust such a creature. You would be wiser to emulate Karhl's approach. Seven days of respecting her boundaries, and she is already comfortable with his *moderated* attention."

And there they were bound to disagree again, Dryden pointing out Karhl's obvious flaw. "But she has not taken him into her body. Another should have been chosen. Karhl reminds her too greatly of the dead Axirlan... Sigil resists out of loyalty to her former lover and places herself at risk by refusing to mate him."

The outcome of Karhl's wisdom, Sovereign admired. His Brother was clever. "And now she is coming here... of her own free will. She is coming to me so that her new esteem for Karhl can prosper. She is coming to me so I might be used as the instrument to deaden her compulsion—a desperate attempt not to tarnish something fragile with the Lord Commander that she does not understand. And so you see, when she chooses to lay with Karhl, it will be only because she desires to." The last words were almost bitter. "How fortunate he is."

The arch of Dryden's eyebrows went as understanding dawned. "Was that his strategy all along?"

"Of course it was." Squinting at the flash off the skyline, Sovereign saw the awaited cruiser descend through the upper atmospheric storm. "Karhl will be the first she loves. Remember that, should you think to challenge your superior's wisdom. The Lord Commander has succeeded where your aggression would have ended with the woman devouring your heart—literally." Sharp and threatening, the Emperor turned on his Brother and growled, "That is a lesson you may add to canon for all Adherents to witness and follow."

The vessel sped nearer, the High Adherent grinning as if he had not heard his Emperor's final warning. "She comes."

Sovereign had placed his faith well.

The Emperor found Sigil dressed in the black leathers of modified Irdesian uniform. Symbolic white paint smeared from her eyes, chalking her forehead, to mat into tightly bound hair. Intricate markings ran down her neck, warning she claimed the highest possible rank, that she was a warrior, and incredibly dangerous.

How the Lord Commander had convinced her to wear high military apparel, Sovereign could not imagine. Nor could he have anticipated the hungry look she bestowed his direction the instant his female caught his scent on the wind.

Even with the massive moon rising behind her, everything was going so well.

Sigil strode from the vessel—Karhl at her side, Arden at her back—and exercised no hesitation in meeting the Irdesian Emperor on the ramparts of his bastion. Her attention was not on the city her people had conquered, the gathering of Brothers at Sovereign's back, or even the chill in the air. It was on the new eye sitting pretty in Sovereign's skull.

As if her pride stung, it seemed she had no interest in stating her reasons for coming. Instead, Sigil hardly blinked, breathed a bit too hard, and smashed her lips against his the moment his mouth parted in greeting.

Her reaction seemed too perfect—the impatient tug of her hands in his hair, the way she growled for more when Sovereign's tongue pushed in to taste her. She pressed against him for more, even began to reach for his belt as if unwilling to wait another moment before he might thrust inside her.

Right here, before his Brothers, she was showing her favor, her desire.

Sovereign could not be more thrilled.

But it ended abruptly, Sigil suddenly frozen, eyes staring forward but seeing nothing.

He spoke to her glassy eyed expression, caressed her cheek. "Welcome to Irdesi, to your home, Sigil."

She hadn't registered his greeting. Instead Sigil shoved Sovereign away, hissing, "Do you hear that?"

Chapter 5

It felt as if her blood had turned to sand. It scratched every vein, every artery, with each pump of her heart. It *burned*.

She had come, dressed in their vile clothes, painted, promised things.

She came to the hideous city she'd viewed from the shuttle's view port. She had even wasted no time pretending there was a need for pleasantries. Right there on the gangway, she would use him, drain him of seed, and walk away with her pride intact.

The shreds of her pride that remained, at least.

But there was a sound that entrusted her body's mission. The man who tasted of honey and spice, didn't seem to hear the scrape of an unhinged mind. He just petted her cheek and smiled.

Sovereign was suddenly much less interesting.

Opening her mind, listening closely, she ground her teeth.

Something wasn't right. Something *mentally stank* like weeks old carrion rotting in the sun. And that something was the craggy soldier standing at attention amongst Sovereign's elites.

He was no different than the others flanking the walkway from ship to palace. Eyes forward, shoulders at attention, he maintained the stillness of his fellow Converts. But elite Converts of that level did not sing inside with the same furious need for violence toward Sovereign that she did.

It only took a tick of time and a blur of movement, and Sigil stood before the offensive mind—the human who dared covet revenge, who thought murder toward the Emperor.

That would never do. Sovereign was hers to kill.

Hers.

She'd startled the soldier by taking his beefy throat into her clutches and effortlessly hoisting him high. His toes fought to scrape the ground as Sigil roared, "YOU REALLY THINK YOU COULD TAKE SOVEREIGN'S LIFE? YOU CANNOT EVEN GET OUT OF MY GRIP."

The human did try, fruitlessly beating at her arm, his face growing purple.

Madness broke out on the causeway.

She ignored it.

Planting a foot, Sigil reared back to throw the unwelcome competition off the lofty walkway, eager to enjoy the view of his body plummeting down to break upon the stones below. But an arm circled her middle, throwing her off balance.

Her mind twisted and raged that another thought to interfere.

If she could not throw the human, she would tear him to pieces instead. Yet when she tried to break the man's arm, Sigil only found her hand restrained.

Demands were growled at her ear. "Release the traitor, young one."

Release what? The bleeding throat she dug her nails into? Her toy?

Possessive of her prey, confused, hungry, fighting to regain control of her limbs, it took the strength of more Brothers than Sigil could see before she was forced to unwillingly drop the human. Then lips were on hers, a delicious bitten tongue in her mouth far more pleasing than the feel of coppery human blood on her fingertips.

She drank of him, of Sovereign, and forgot about the Convert gasping for breath at her feet.

Sovereign was stroking her neck in a way that felt sublime, cooing that she could be calm, that she had done well. That she was safe. Orders were shouted, Karhl's deep rumble coarse in the background.

The Lord Commander demanded the prisoner be healed and dissected piece by piece until the corruption was identified and purged from the ranks.

Over and over came the foul term, *Unsalvageable*.

When Sovereign gave her a moment of breath, when his grip on her nape tightened to the point her body was forced into an unnatural stillness, Sigil saw what she'd done. The human lived, Arden single-handedly subduing the raving Convert while more soldiers poured out of the grey walled citadel.

Shrinking once her nape was released, she scampered away. The large mass of the Lord

Commander came sharply against her back. His arms circled her middle as if to offer shelter or restraint. Her choice.

His attention went to her leg. "You're wounded."

Was she?

Her eyes followed his to find skewered straight through the limb was a bloody blade. Considering the angle, it was lodged in bone. But she felt nothing.

And she felt nothing because it was poisoned with a toxin that would kill any human, but do little more than make her leg useless for a time. "Certax."

Kneeling, Sovereign braced her leg and yanked out the dagger. Gripping the hilt to the point his fingers turned white, he said, "Karhl is going to escort you to your rooms where there are no Converts and you will be utterly safe. Do you understand me?"

The soldier had only stabbed her in desperation. She was in no danger. No, that human's song of murder was only for the Emperor.

"How did a Convert of that level become able to resist? What is that word you all whisper? Unsalvageable?" And why the fuck had she rushed to kill something so weak when it did little more than think a threat toward Sovereign and brandish a knife smeared with useless poison?

He came to his feet. "You need to go inside, beloved."

Her face fell, full of disbelief. "You don't know…"

Absolute, dangerous, Sovereign let a fraction of what he was truly capable of ooze into the air between them. "I have ways of finding out."

This was not why she'd crossed space. She had not come here to be embroiled in Irdesian schemes. "I came here—"

Instantly softer, the Emperor offered reassurance. "I know why you came here. I will not leave you waiting long."

She wanted it over now. "I have waited five days."

Sovereign took a small step nearer, running his thumb over her mouth. "Seven days, Sigil. And you are doing well. I am very proud of your progress."

Unacceptable. He needed to fuck her and get it over with so she could leave Irdesian lunacy and return to her solitude surrounded by water. "I don't want a pat on the head!"

Cold outrage mutilated the beauty of Sovereign's expression, the thick command of his words chilled to the bone. "Sigil, you will go into the safety of your rooms at this very moment."

Her useless leg dragged over the ground, Karhl ushering her physically free of the mad swarm of Brothers and elite Convert soldiers, out of the dark, and into a thicker cloying blackness.

Chapter 6

He had kept her waiting, leaving Sigil frustrated and sequestered in an unfamiliar place. Even so, Sovereign had not expected to find her as she was.

"What is she doing?" His frown sat tight under a minute scowl.

"Drinking," Arden answered, looking through the translucent golden partitions that surrounded the great table in the Imperial Consort's quarters.

Sovereign was not amused. "And Karhl has allowed this?"

"Not at first." The golden one shrugged, eyeing the female sitting alone at a table cut from a single slab of onyx, her fingertips tracing over etchings filled with bronze. "But she started to cry, and he gave her what she wanted."

Karhl stood like an over-muscled fixture beside where the female sat, pouring herself another serving of rare Tessan Fire Spirits.

Sigil had tried to wipe off the white paint crusting her forehead, tried to free herself from the bindings in her hair, and had clearly shredded a good deal of her clothes.

As if armed with the secrets of the universe, Arden smirked, peeking toward Sovereign from the corner of his eye. "I don't think she can move her leg."

"Is that why she cried?" The Emperor spoke lowly, his strategy for her arrival ruined beyond repair. His disappointment was intense.

"No. She wants to go back to *Xevdrik Anni*—to her Seasons and her Jerla. Karhl told her that would be impossible; explaining how the tale of what took place on the landing would have spread throughout the city. Now that Converts know the Imperial Consort has awoken, and until her position is established, she is unsafe away from the Brotherhood's seat of power."

Sovereign's crossed arms flexed, internally raging to find Sigil so unhappy. "He was correct."

Setting a manicured hand on his Brother's shoulder, Arden explained. "She blames you, of course." The quicksilver smirk was back, the Herald shifting his weight the second Sigil reached for an unopened flask. "Upset or no, she does not need that second bottle of spirits, so I am going to go take that away from her. Hopefully Karhl keeps her from drinking my blood instead."

Projecting a light and carefree voice, Arden moved around the partition and into Sigil's line of sight. "Jerla is in transit, Sister. He will be here soon, where you will see that he is safe."

Hardly above a growl, Sigil snarled. "He will think he is being taken to the sands."

The fresh bottle was swiped out of her reach, Arden tutting. "No one will let him think such a thing. And when he arrives, your boy will know he can trust you."

"You give me that bottle, Arden, or I will rip off your arm and take it from your bleeding corpse!"

Dancing back so quickly her eyes could hardly follow, the Herald chuckled. "Are you going to hop one-legged after me?"

No. It appeared she would use her newfound ability to exercise what Sovereign deemed *useful psionics*. Her attempt was not graceful, her sad lack for subtlety yanking more objects near her than just one lean Herald. But in the end, she had the bottle, Karhl had been soundly pegged in the head, and Arden was no longer grinning.

Intervening in the mayhem, Sovereign rounded the partition. "Arden, leave."

Bowing, the Herald bypassed the mess Sigil's unpracticed mental tug had piled on the floor and exited the chamber.

"Precious Sigil, you have my apologies. This was not how I envisioned introducing you to the palace, the family quarters"—Sovereign's eyes went to the bottle at her mouth—"or my cellar."

Swallowing loudly, Sigil rubbed her lips together. "If I had not attacked your soldier, would I have been allowed to return to the Water Palace?"

The issue might as well be dealt with directly. "No."

Regret, the sense she did not believe him, sat open on her face. "Why?"

"This is your home, Sigil." He rested his hand atop hers. "And it has been waiting for you, just as I have."

She was beginning to grow visually upset. There was even a hint more tears might fall when she complained, "You saw what happened. I was not more than three steps off the cruiser!"

"What happened?" Sovereign smiled, projecting pride in what she'd done. "You uncovered a *Soshiia* rebel agent long before I believe he intended to act. My gratitude is yours."

After a full-mouthed swallow, Sigil demanded an explanation. "What is Soshiia?"

"Had you read the journals Arden wrote for you, you would know, and spare me a lengthy explanation. Fortunately, they are being transferred here, along with your other things."

Narrowing her eyes, threatening him in every aspect of her demeanor, Sigil hissed. "I don't want what I came here for. Not anymore… I just want to be left alone!"

Sovereign nodded, going so far as to remove his touch from her hand. "I understand."

Outright suspicion shone on her face. "You… you do?"

"Drink your fire spirits. Karhl can show you your sleeping chamber when you're tired. Your desire for solitude will be respected, though I expect Jerla will want to see you when he arrives."

Wiping her mouth on the back of her hand, Sigil took a deep breath. "Jerla is welcome."

"As you wish, beloved." Nothing more was offered. Sovereign stood, bowing just as Arden had and left the room.

Sovereign's implanted communicator relayed there were greater issues than Sigil drinking herself into a stupor. Arden awaited him at the gates to the family wing, and required the presence of the Emperor at once.

Leaving her was wise. Karhl would tend her, her confidence would return, and the sight of Jerla would add normalcy to an unstable situation. But there was one approaching, one who would go as far as to break down the door if Sovereign did not intervene.

An expression of hate passed over the Emperor's face. He glared as if he could see through the walls, beyond the barred entry of Sigil's wing, all the way to where Lord Commander Tiburon awaited, his faction of the Brotherhood behind him.

Navigating the corridors and antechambers, Sovereign came to the massive double doors and motioned for them to be opened. Once he stepped through, they were sealed like a vault, leaving the Emperor dwarfed before the great portal.

Even with the Emperor standing at the threshold, Lord Commander Tiburon's eyes burned only toward the Herald standing in defense of the passage. He spoke, allowing hate to saturate his threats. "If you believe you can command me, Arden, I will gladly remind you that a Herald does not outrank a Lord Commander. I could crush you, as Sigil could crush you. That you were tasked with her keeping is laughable."

Tiburon had arrived fully armored, armed even, his shaved head cocked so the long scar that ran in a diagonal over his eye caught the light. Those cold eyes cut to the silent Emperor, and it seemed violence was only a hair's breadth away. "Is it as Arden claims? You would deny me the company of our Sigil?"

Sovereign smiled, the gesture anything but welcoming. "Her demeanor is agitated. She requested solitude."

A nasty grin came to the face of one of the most aggressive of their kind. "I will fuck her calm."

Arden interposed, standing between the two large warriors as if his lesser mass might hold them from tearing one another apart. "Karhl is with her. She'll only accept attention from him."

A disgusted throat noise came from Tiburon, his face screwed up. "A Brother who can't bring himself to spread her legs for her own good? Sigil would not have been in harm's way on the ramparts had she been mounted and subdued properly before arrival. Had she arrived *of sound mind,* she could have told us of the conspiracy without unveiling the agent. An opportunity to track the origins of the Soshiia infection has been wasted.”

“That would have been ideal, yes. But you forget, Lord Commander Tiburon” —the title was spoken in full to emphasize that the aggressor ranked below the calm-faced Emperor— “that she is not our ally as of yet. What makes you think she would have spoken a word to assist our empire? What makes you think the Soshiia might not have tried to seduce her with promises of our demise? Now they will fear her. It is better this way.”

“You coddle her too much.” Tiburon ran a finger over his metal filled scar—a mark he wore with great pride—licking his lips as he glanced to the door separating him from the female. “It is why she does not respect you, and why you cannot bring her into a fertile cycle. Sigil requires a firmer hand.”

The grave insult drew a low growl deep from Sovereign’s chest.

With a vicious smile breaking across his face, Tiburon snickered under his breath. Turning, he motioned for the Brothers at his back to retreat. “When it’s my turn, she won’t be able to walk for a week. I’ll do what you can’t, and inspire our little slut into heat. It might be your seed that gets her fat, but all will know the first daughter is really mine.”

Hours spent torturing the Soshiia infiltrator did little to calm the rage within the Emperor, but it had dampened it enough. As with all other rebel agents, the human died giving little information.

It burned, just as it confirmed Tiburon's earlier taunt.

In many ways, the Lord Commander had been correct. Sigil might not have outright attacked the human had she not been on the cusp of regression. And leaving her in that state was a risk—an even greater risk now that the Brotherhood must concede a spy had climbed through the upper ranks unnoticed.

It should not have been possible.

Traversing her vacant living areas, Sovereign found shreds of clothes left discarded in a trail toward her sleeping chamber—breadcrumbs to follow.

Entering the room, he found her sleeping, tucked in the great bed he'd commissioned be carved by the finest artisans of the human worlds eighty years prior. *Gillatern* Forest's largest tree rose to touch cathedral ceilings, the branching sculpture detailed with birds in flight, bedecked with renditions of the empire's most beautiful flowers, hung with banners of pure white draped against so much black lacquered wood. Seeming innocent in sleep, Sigil lay naked, white paint matting the roots of her hair.

She was not alone.

His consort was embraced in the arms of Karhl, pressed to her back as he stroked her gently, the Lord Commander unabashedly enjoying the moment of intimacy between them.

"She must be mated now, though I anticipate it will anger her that it was not on her terms," Sovereign grunted, eyeing the line of her spine as he began to strip and approach. Once naked, he crawled between the covers, pressing close to the woman who smelled of moss and honey liquor.

Pale, dangerous fingers carded through her long, silvery hair. Karhl regarded the sleeping female, studying her intently. "Her transition was complex. Hours ago I stood defensive of imminent attack. Sigil's eyes had tracked my every movement. She'd even begun to cycle her psionics. Had her leg been fully functional, I am certain I would have been forced to restrain her."

"And?'

"Jerla's arrival was well-timed." Karhl met the Emperor's eye. "One look at the boy, at his skittish body language, and she became a lamb."

Watching his beloved, longing greatly to reach out and run his thumb over the line formed between her brows, Sovereign sighed. "Lamb is not a title she would appreciate."

"True…" Head bent, Karhl nuzzled the female's hair. Inhaling deeply, he closed his eyes.

Sovereign watched the rise and fall of his Consort's breaths, having missed sharing his nights with the woman he adored. "Tiburon demands access. For her own good she must be fully stable."

Karhl's counterpart held great power in the Empire—Lord Commander Tiburon had a strong right to the woman burrowing beautifully against the

Emperor in her sleep, and there was nothing either male could do to stop him.

The lightest of touches traced over soft, parted lips, Sovereign calling to her. "My precious Sigil."

With a deep breath, she came awake.

Finding herself trapped between the naked bodies of two aroused men, her gaze grew extremely wary. But unless she climbed over one of them, Sigil would not be able to evade.

He didn't want to fight her. He didn't want to force her.

But he needed her to be sound.

Acting before she might consider full retreat, Sovereign pressed a kiss to a frowning mouth.

Whether it was a complaint, pure surprise, or resigned acceptance, her squeak was lost under the pressure of his lips. Her stiffness went ignored as he cupped a breast and give a rough tweak to soft nipple.

She arched, as he expected her to, more of her jumbled words twisted by his tongue.

Karhl was equally relentless. Reaching around, his fingers dove between her closed thighs.

Her next squeal was not exactly one of protest.

While his Brother teased Sigil's clit, Sovereign found himself caught in his own brand of resentment. Jealousy warred with his desire. Even so, feeling his Brother's hand between their bodies, knowing what he was doing to their female, made his cock throb.

It's not as if he had never shared women with his Brothers before Sigil was born. He had, many, many times. But this was different. This was *her*.

There was no other option. This was the way it had to be, and if it took Karhl's practiced attention to foster the kind of noises his beloved was making now, then so be it.

Tongue in Sigil's mouth, Sovereign pulled at her nipple again, stretched out the flesh, and twisted. He knew she loved it, knew it was more than Karhl's touch that had scented the air with the smell of her growing excitement.

She responded to him, no matter if she wanted to or not.

When he released her abused breast, Sovereign gave the bouncing flesh a sharp slap. Leaving her lips to lavish attention on her chest, but cautious not to give her voice to reject what had to be done, he put his fingers in her mouth, and keep her tongue occupied.

Like a trained pleasure slave, she sucked his digits, a pink tongue coming to play and lick.

But the woman's eyes remained closed, as if she might deny who gave her pleasure so long as she refused to look.

Sovereign understood exactly what this was.

Rebellion. And it didn't deter him in the slightest.

She might not want to look at what they did, but he could see that she heard.

Lips at her ear, he growled, "I'm going to fuck you. I'm going to make you come. And I'm going to fill you up with what you need."

Nothing.

He bit her nipple when she refused to respond.

The feel of his teeth drew her to groan. He did it again to the underside of her breast, bit hard enough to bruise.

Arching her back, moaning, her legs fell open, and Karhl's hand dived in to play with more than just her clit. Two knuckles deep, the Lord Commander's fingers disappeared inside her, came out with a wet slurp, and wiggled right back in.

It seemed he too was intent on making her hear every last sound.

"Karhl…"

It was a dagger in Sovereign's heart hearing her sigh another's name.

Maybe he was pushing too hard, demanding too much in his temper over the Soshiia agent?

Amnesty, mercy, love.

He could give her those things, and suffer in silence until she was willing to acknowledge what they both knew on a cellular level—that he might share her, but she was *his*. In the meantime, he would let her pretend this moment was only between herself and the Lord Commander.

In fact, he'd make sure that's all she would see if it would please her.

As if of the same mind, Karhl got to his knees when Sovereign took Sigil by the hair. The Emperor pulled her up, turned her from his body, and pushed her mouth toward the Lord Commander's swollen organ.

The Imperial Consort fell upon that pierced cock as if ravenous.

Based off reports, she most likely was. Ravenous, that is.

It had been seven days…

Sigil swallowed the pierced cock down as if it were nothing, Sovereign noting the wide-eyed surprise on his Brother's face at some unseen thing she did with her tongue. The large, pale warrior even gasped her name as if after all his centuries of life and multitude of sexual experiences, he'd never felt anything as wondrous.

Again, envy bloomed in Sovereign's heart. And it was that envy, that dark covetousness that made him claw at female hips, that urged him to line up his cock for the kill. He thrust so roughly into that sopping pussy, that the woman gagged around his Brother's erection.

Sovereign held her like that, fist bunched in her hair, abusing her cunt… and knew that even if she did not wish to acknowledge his part in this expression of lechery, that she loved every last slap of his hips against her ass.

The slippery proof of her excitement dripped down his thigh, shone against the pulsing veins of his cock when he pulled out just enough to see himself plunge right back in.

Karhl was a bit more delicate. Still, the two of them fucked her in unison, occasionally watching the other, both deliriously caught up in assertive pleasure.

And Sigil… she was moaning around a fat, pierced cock for more.

It was as reports claimed, and his more volatile experiences on Pax confirmed—she liked to be used and debased.

Hurt.

When Sovereign squeezed her hips hard enough to leave bruises, she crooned. When Karhl began to roar and thrust impatiently down her throat, she gushed.

But to see her enjoy the drag of Karhl's metal studs over her tongue, to watch her enthusiastically taste the organ she had denied herself at the Water Palace… it inspired a different sin in Sovereign than lust.

Yet his cock grew ever harder, more swollen, painfully ready to explode.

The Lord Commander's balls had drawn up tight, Sovereign watching as his Brother reached down to knead his sack. Seeing his Brother come, listening to the slurp and suck of his woman swallowing every drop of tangy liquid, undid him.

The Emperor went from vicious to crazed.

The hand still fisted in her hair drew her back until her lips popped off Karhl's softening organ. His other hand came to her throat.

And back she went, yanked upward until her back met Sovereign's chest, and it was only his body sliding against her sweat-slicked skin.

He needed her to come on his cock. He NEEDED her to be covered in his semen, his smell, his love.

Bouncing her on his dick, teeth at her neck, he reeled.

Her womb… he longed to fill her womb with so many daughters. To have a piece of him grow inside her, stretch her belly, engorge her breasts with milk.

This is why he existed, why he sacrificed. For her. For their future.

Karhl seemed to collect himself, to sit up from where he'd fallen forward on his hands, and to consider what was at stake in the moment. It was as if they were of a like mind. His white head dipped, the man pressing his lips to their shared female. He laved her breasts, raising them up to his mouth. He accepted her scratches and screams.

And then the Lord Commander moved even lower.

As if entranced, he watched her sweet pussy, watched it glisten and be stretched by the determined aggression of his Emperor's cock.

The man licked his lips.

Catching the metal rod that decorated her hood with the tip of his tongue, Karhl gave her a lick.

When she jerked, he groaned and gave her all of his tongue. It swept over that swollen nub, her stretched labia, careless of the plunging cock he brushed and the salty taste of his Emperor's excitement. He did not let up no matter how their shared female squirmed and tried to get away.

The woman began to moan so loudly Sovereign was certain every Brother in the palace could hear.

They would recognize what was done here.

They would envy her desire.

At that thought, Sovereign smiled wickedly against his caught female's neck.

He could feel her body shuck its restraint under the onslaught of two eager lovers. It started with a pulsating undulation that squeezed his cock from base to tip. Her legs shook where they straddled his thighs, her head thrown back on a scream as she begged them to end it.

Her cunt drew so tight Sovereign was certain her body was trying to squeeze the life from him.

So, life he gave her.

All he'd been holding back began to usher forth in a massive release. From the base of his spine perfection surged, led to greater heights when Karhl unexpectedly cupped Sovereign's sack as he had done his own, kneading the tender flesh just enough to amplify orgasm beyond anything the Emperor had ever known.

Sovereign saw white, he saw black… he saw the perfect red of bloody victory as he bit Sigil's spine and filled their bride with fertile seed.

It took her some time to realize Sovereign cradled her against his chest, that both Karhl and the Emperor were speaking to her, praising such a giving performance.

She was beyond breath, panting in a way only hours on Swelter's silks could incite.

"Beloved." Nipping her raw nape between words, Sovereign promised her, "Every day will be better. You will never be lonely. You will never be frightened. This faith you have shown me, I will pay it back tenfold."

It was Karhl who saw her expression constrict, watched her lips losing their softness when too much thinking wrecked her calm. He took her chin in a rough pinch, assuring she listened to every word. "You are not on Condor. Handlers cannot tell you how to feel. Neither can Sovereign. Neither can I. And neither can your corroding programming. From this day forward, you must think for yourself."

"You are free, beloved." Sovereign rolled his hips to remind her, to press his liquid offering deeper. "That is what I offer you."

Her whole body ached.

Outside the windows, the sun was rising. When the light hit the floor, Sovereign eased from her womb, brushing lips over her knotted brow as he excused himself to prepare for court. He left her spent and tangled in the sheets to consider all that had been done. Karhl followed suit, offering his own farewell. Kissing her moody pout away, he departed to attend to his own duties.

With the Emperor and Lord Commander gone, Arden waited at the door, an audience she'd failed to notice in the pleasure of the last pairing. Smiling, the Herald took in her disheveled nudity, drew her from the bed, and pulled her deeper into the mountain.

Sun disappeared, fire lit catacombs offering a sense of depth until the beauty of a natural spring bubbled up under lamplight.

While Sigil scanned the vast cave, Arden shoved her into the steaming water, laughing even as he stripped his tunic to join her.

Splashing, chasing the sputtering woman through the pool, Arden incited games Sigil didn't quite understand, coaxing out a predator's love for hunt and evasion.

She would give chase; he would disappear, splashing her from behind.

In no time at all, the brilliant Herald coaxed out the first laugh any survivor of Cataclysm had ever heard their female sing.

"What are the Soshiia?"

Arden glanced up from where he'd placed his journals in an alcove. The golden one tilted up the corner of his lips, seemed to think on his answer, and sighed. "Every society has their anarchist."

That wasn't exactly the answer Sigil had been looking for. Scowling, she looked at his books and said, "Sovereign told me your journals told the story."

Frowning, returning to his work, Arden admitted, "I suppose they do."

Staring at the long plait of golden hair that hung down the entire length of his spine, Sigil grunted, "And if I want to know, I have to read? You won't just tell me."

"It's a complicated explanation requiring a detailed understanding of our history. Anything I might tell you in casual conversation would lack the necessary depth of the truth."

Leaning back on the red damask couch, Sigil understood. "So it's something terrible… I will blame the Empire for it unless I understand the *why of it*. And to understand the why of it, I have to commit to absorbing a lot more than just the story of a rebel group."

"Maybe."

He was teasing her; she could sense the playfulness, and could not help but smirk. "I thought you were supposed to be on my side."

Utterly serious, Arden turned so she might see his fervent expression. "I am on your side, Sigil. I will always be on your side."

Pointing to the volumes, Sigil sighed. "Give me one."

Pleased, Arden pulled a red bound book from the shelf and held it toward the woman. "You have enough time before Dryden and Corths arrive, to read at least the initial installment."

She'd only shared evening meals with the High Adherents at the Water Palace. Never had they come to her rooms midday. Unhappy with the thought, she ground her teeth and opened the cover.

"It would break their hearts to see you scowl so at the prospect of their company. They love you greatly, Sister, and are only coming to assure your attendants behave in accordance with the honor of their position."

Now she was really annoyed. "What?"

"Each Convert woman was hand selected—reared—to please you."

"Slavery is illegal in the Empire."

Arden laughed as if she'd said something cute. "Believe me, the females are willing, eager even. For humans with no military skill, who lack influential bloodlines, there is little opportunity to advance. Considering your needs, it is an ideal arrangement on both sides." He had a further point to make, "No son, no daughter, or anyone tied to a human house of standing could possibly be in your intimacy without upsetting the balance of power. So, several of your Brothers have taken it upon themselves to cultivate your retainers from the lowest tribes, sending them as gifts."

It seemed the Brothers played at politics with each other just as the humans did... all seeking favor. "Why would I need attendants?"

"To dress you, bathe you, amuse you, and even die for you should the situation require. If you want silence, they will be mute. If you desire court gossip, they will disclose anything they uncover."

She shook her head. "They would be loyal to the Brother who'd raised them, directing their conversation to uplift the one who gave them the position."

There was no advantage in lying about such a point. "Fortunately, you are an empath and can use such an extraordinary sense to protect yourself from the unworthy."

He had earned Sigil's attention, the female sitting up on her elbows. "Are you warning me against your Brothers?"

"As I said, I am on your side."

Narrowing her eyes, Sigil cocked her head and looked hard at the man putting away trinkets like a servant. "Just how fragile is your compact with one another?"

Smiling, beautiful, Arden reached forward and ran a finger over her jaw. "Everything you need to know is in my journals."

It was obvious how badly Arden wanted her to read his account of things, how manipulative the Herald was behaving. That did not stop her from lowering her eyes to the page and starting at the beginning.

Chapter 7

The sensation of thick cosmetic dragging over her skin was unpleasant; how they tinted every last ounce of flesh, pointless in Sigil's opinion. But she stood stagnant while five women, all so different it seemed they'd been chosen as art, painted her body white.

They made her a blank canvas.

The attendants were quiet, focused on their work, just as they had been each time they had invaded her space. The Convert females, Sigil found, were harmless. Weak. They behaved as complaisant dolls, wandering about in a fixed internal state of awe. But she wasn't sure if it was her they were in awe of, or the High Adherent overseeing the dressing of the Imperial Consort.

The women wouldn't meet Sigil's watchful eyes, too busy in the artful application of inky script flowing down her limbs. They were too busy painting a new face over the one she already owned. But they did send furtive glances toward Dryden, as if gauging his appraisal.

He, apparently, was the gatekeeper to a position of high desirability. He was also exacting, no matter how softly he smiled. Eyes aglow—done up in full regalia far more ornamental than the military uniform of Brotherhood soldiers or the tailored tunics of Heralds—his short-cropped hair hidden under a miter etched with the same symbols a doe-eyed attendant painted between Sigil's breasts. It was nothing compared to the layers of fabric they would pull over her, constructed gowns the attendants would lace and tighten, layer and hook. And once they were done, all clothing would be removed, an hour's effort wasted.

Sigil did not like restrictive garments. She didn't like the paint, the jewels, the weight of sunburst headpieces, or the taste of black lacquer on her lips.

More importantly, Sigil refused to leave her rooms, making the dressing unnecessary—mere practice for *future* excursions.

Three days she'd remained sequestered. For three days Dryden had tried to tempt her out, offering to show her the palace, the gardens, the tombs where her fallen Brothers slept, anything he thought might entice. Arden had remained neutral on the topic, always near, the Herald's arms crossed over his chest and a sly smirk on his mouth as he watched the procedure.

Sigil suspected the Herald remained silent because Arden was getting what *he* wanted. She spent her waking hours reading his vast collection of journals—much to her frustration. Even after ten volumes, she had yet to come across mention of the word 'Soshiia,' but she could name every last Brother who had died since the formation of the Empire. She could list battles, and noble houses. She knew the names of Imperial planets, how they were captured, if they were converted or slaughtered.

Sovereign had not commented on the matter of her isolation. Nor had Karhl. Perhaps they condoned it. Sigil didn't know, and she didn't want to know.

All in all, time in the Imperial Palace was similar to her seasons on the Water Planet. Always food waited in a hall austere in its black stone and bronze veined walls. Rooms were filled with items collected to entertain her. But where the Water Palace soaked rooms in sun, there was scant natural light in these new vaulted caverns. Every room faded into the shadows, every space seemingly carved out of the mountains of Irdesi Prime.

But there had been a glowing room she'd seen upon being dragged in by Karhl days ago. A domed ceiling of stained glass, tier after tier of arcades circling up like a cathedral—the gallery at the heart of the family rooms, she'd been told. Rooms for her children. For her children's children. For visiting Brothers invited inside. All empty at present. Never used.

It was through that vast space she'd have to pass to reach the massive armored gates that separated her from the remainder of the palace.

Seeing Sigil lost in thought during another session of dressing, Dryden, again, made a play for her attention. "Reports indicate Jerla is responding well to his immunity fortification. He may wake tomorrow."

The boy had only been allowed to see her once upon his arrival to this human cesspool. After a brief reunion, Arden had carried the strangely lethargic boy away. Sigil had been denied the child since, left only with a hologram projection so she might watch Jerla's sleeping response to the seemingly necessary, invasive vaccines all Tessans had to undergo to survive amidst the Convert worlds. Unlike her, he lacked an advanced immune system, Jerla made weaker still from the subpar environment of his hatchling years.

Her eyes went back to the projection, watching the physician attending the boy. It was the same Brother who had attended her in her sleep. The High Adherent, Corths, sat with the child, monitoring his status, his vitals, beefing up a fragile system so her *toy* might be returned to her.

That was how they treated her Jerla—as an extension of whatever made Sigil happy.

In the Brotherhood's eyes, he was a tool. If that were not the case, Arden, the one charged with tending him on the Water Planet, would have been with him and not with her. His affection was not sincere. The thought made Sigil bitter, made her narrow her eyes at the Herald.

"Are you feeling unwell?" They were the first words Arden had spoken since the attendants' arrival.

Movement came from the hologram. Sigil looked back to see Corths take the boy's hand and pat it as he spoke. The image lacked audio, so she could not make out what was being said.

Arden, it seemed, understood. "He's telling your boy a story."

Her question was harsh. "Why?"

A golden head cocked, the Herald taking measure of their female slowly. "Corths held your hand often in the decades you slept. He told the same stories to you. When he did, your vitals steadied, your brain waves calmed, and you rested more soundly."

Sigil offered a hiss. "I don't much like your stories."

The room went quiet, the females who had been combing something viscous through all her hair, who had been sculpting the clay-like mass into intricate fans about her skull, stepped back.

"I ordered Corths to attend him." Sovereign slipped into their company, a commanding presence that diminished all others. "There is no better physician in the Empire, beloved. Nor will your Brother leave the child's side until the therapy is complete. You do not need to fear for your boy."

Only half dressed, half painted, and with only half her hair attended to, Sigil stepped off the dais.

There was a smile, a caution in Sovereign's tone. "All Tessans who come to Irdesi must undergo the same treatment. Even seclusion those first hours was not enough to keep him from growing sick in the presence of aggressive microorganisms. The bacteria here, the viruses, are not compatible with their unaltered systems. Jerla will be made stronger for this."

"He never got sick on Pax."

"He was constantly sick on Pax, riddled with parasites and tumors that squeezed his digestive tract. They were removed and treated while you slept:

while he slept waiting for you. Had they not been, he would have died in a matter of years, no matter where he'd been *freed*."

Then what of all the other children she had set free? Had they too been eaten from the inside out? Sigil's face one of horror at such thoughts, she swallowed and looked like she might be sick. "Then why was this procedure not conducted then? Why now that I've been dragged here?"

"We were not sure if you desired to keep him, or if he was to be sent to a Tessan world. The gift of survival on our planets is not given to foreigners. Only ambassadors granted Imperial approval are offered such a boon. And, they are not permitted to leave the Empire, ever."

Pacing nearer the Emperor, Sigil measured what she'd heard. "Jerla will not be allowed to leave?"

Sovereign reached out to twist a decorated bit of Sigil's hair between his fingers. "Do you wish to send him away?"

"No."

He gave her hair a playful tug. "Have you not accepted him into your family?"

What did that matter? "…Yes."

"Then what is the issue that upsets you?"

A jumble of arguments banged around in her skull. "Once grown, he might not wish to stay. One day he'll desire a mate. How will he find her? What if he grows unafraid of the sands and wishes to pilgrimage?”

“Your chosen child will not leave you, Sigil. Tessan family bonds are distinct. As for a mate, he may choose a human. Otherwise, there are years yet to solve that riddle.” Sovereign edged closer, slipped an arm around her middle, and let his lips tease her white, painted neck. “If he wakes and sees you so unsteady, it will worry him. Jerla needs you to remain collected. You’ll have him back soon enough.”

His mouth so close, Sigil knew he was threatening her with a bite. Every time she twitched, it was as if one of them thought she might pop.

But she *was* fine! Sovereign had fucked her often enough to assure it. Sigil was fine, hadn’t even killed a single attendant or so much as slapped Arden.

Life in Irdesi’s capital made her skin crawl.

It had been only three days, but it felt like eons, like grit under her fingernails she couldn’t pick out.

The damned journals were a part of her frustration, that much was true. The information Arden, Sovereign—all of them—wanted her to absorb from the *Histories* plagued her. And for good reason. There was inconsistency in the stories, facts recorded wrongly that made no sense to the female who’d lived what Arden thought to recreate in text.

Either they were testing her, lying to themselves, or… they didn’t know the truth.

The first volume was the most flawed. In decisive script, the entirety of the book detailed her

103

childhood, initially correct to a point Sigil found it greatly disturbing to relive in reading. And then the tale grew blaringly inaccurate. The chronicle outlined her incarceration on Condor—her routine, meals, behaviors, training—all leading up to her violent escape. From that point, several Brothers' accounts were written. Karhl's version was there, his explanation of how a child had almost killed him, cautioning heavily against anyone approaching without a cage already constructed to contain the little girl. Arden had been there too. He had seen her from a distance when she ran through Sector C. The former assassin had given chase, only to be crushed by debris when Sigil began tearing down the walls of the compound. On and on the stories went, piecing together the first moments of the Alliance's fall into a timeline the Brotherhood could trace and agree upon—their profile of her behaviors haunting.

Her memory of that day, even though she'd been caught in a rage, was precise. She remembered hearing her mother's mental screams. Sigil remembered that first burning wave of childlike panic distorting the walls of her cell. Psionics clicked into place, and it was easy, so very easy, to enact long-imagined vengeance.

That's where the book began to fill with outright lies. Unwilling to draw attention by staring at one page longer than another, Sigil had continued reading Arden's collection of eyewitness accounts. Then her escape from Condor ended, replaced by boring pages filled with *confirmed* sightings over the decades, suspected places she'd been, interviews with witnesses. A nightmarish psychological profile stared back at her, wherein Sigil was the villain of every story, the bringer of tragedies.

Damaged.

Through all those pages, Sigil was left with an utter lack of progress on her original question.

Who were the Soshiia?

But it seemed that was no longer the only relevant question. Why didn't the journal capture the truth about that last day on Condor? Why did the canon of her breakout claim she was responsible for the death of a potentially valuable human hostage, a female someone else had murdered? Why had the only Brother she'd shared any significant contact with that day omit such an important fact in Arden's histories?

Why should she care?

After all, Sigil was not willingly involved with any of the survivors of Project Cataclysm or their fabricated culture.

Trapped as she was on their ugly planet, surrounded by *them*, how small she'd begun to feel.

Life had once been simple. Fun.

Stuck on Irdesi, with every passing hour Sigil grew more and more dejected.

Only Sovereign could offer distraction. And they both knew what kind of distraction he had in mind.

It was as if they wanted her so bored that she might start to look forward to his company.

She missed Pax more than she could say.

She missed Que.

She tolerated Sovereign.

Sometimes she was even a little afraid of what he could make her feel. Sometimes she forgot that her name was Quinn. Sigil was a title, a designation on a file.

She missed Quinn the most.

It was the oddest sensation, allowing Sovereign to stand so near her, pretending to be unaffected by the immensity of his presence, the changes he'd made to her life—to let him touch her because it was *simpler* than trying to detach his arms from his body.

The truth was, compared to Sovereign, she was meek without her once titanic psionics. Quinn had been unstoppable. Sigil was a kept pet.

Coming to terms with the loss of such uncontrollable, terrible power, was beginning to feel burdensome, not liberating. There was no way out. Were she to fight Sovereign, to fully attack him, he would defeat her every time.

Strong as she was, Sigil was lesser than the humans' overlord.

And Sovereign paid for it. Frustration over such thoughts had cost the Emperor a good deal of blood when he fucked her. Sigil attacked outright, dug in her nails, bit in her frenzy—as if to prove to them both she was strong enough to dislodge him should she want to. When he held her down, when he fought back and gnawed her nape, Sigil came so hard she blanked, and then she'd keep coming until he filled her with that poisoned ejaculate that altered her chemistry.

After the first morning she'd sucked Karhl's pierced cock down her throat, she'd also rejected the Lord Commander's advances—his company—for the last three days. That left her with the constant presence of Arden, who would sometimes just hold her hand, and pretend he could not see her searching out exits. He even pretended he had not seen her cry.

This new person inside her, this acquiescent player on the stage, Sigil didn't know her. This new person was almost always wretched, felt fear, worried. This new person found herself comforted simply being near the creature she hated most... a creature who was stronger than her, who had hurt her, who'd brought more misery into her life, but who could make her feel so very good.

"You feel suffocated." Sovereign spoke as if he could understand her thoughts, rubbing at her nape until wild eyes lost some of their passion. "There is a terrace outside our bedchamber, secluded away from the eyes of any others. Fresh air, the sun, might be a welcome change?"

What terrace? There were no doors beside the vast archway that led to that chamber. There was only more of that jewel-toned, silvery stained glass Sigil could not break.

She'd tried.

Quiet, she let him lead her from the room, through dark halls, to the place where the Emperor had fucked her only hours ago. He waved his hand over the carved wall and it parted, sunlight breaking through a seam so well crafted, Sigil would not have found the portal otherwise.

Back in the dressing chamber, Dryden snarled at Arden, "You are not doing well enough!"

Well enough his ass. Arden was just as frustrated as the Imperial Consort.

Golden eyes snapped to the man squishing black embroidered robes in his pacing. "Sigil hates your contrived pageantry. Your attempt to force our female into the role of the *Adherents'* crafted Imperial Consort bores her. The demigod you feed the masses does not exist, no matter how much you long to parade her about for humans to gawk at."

Outranking the Herald, Dryden lifted his chin and sneered. "What would you have her do? Let her walk the halls naked as she walks these rooms, as she existed in the Water Palace? Her success within the imperium requires assent to politics. Court dress displays power, rank. Centuries lie ahead of her, but her actions now will forever define the tenure of Convert sentiment, of allies' and enemies' regard. Adherents exist to assure her success. It is my duty to see her prosperous!"

"What about her feelings? She is miserable!"

"It is your place to entertain her. If you cannot fulfill your duty, I vote we have you executed and replaced. Tiburon and Karhl will back me in this. Sovereign can be made to do as we see fit."

Grinning, a vein popping out near his temple, Arden warned, "Sigil would never allow it. I am the only one of us she actually likes."

The fourth day Sigil woke to the feel of Sovereign already inside her—his latest trick—so he might mount her before her full physical onslaught might begin. Rolling his hips, grinding to tempt her into sensual pairing, to coax a soft response, drew out a pleasured gasp and a few precious moments of Sigil's compliance. He whispered in her ear that he loved her, fought to keep her between waking and dreaming so she might be taken without her penchant for violence.

Sovereign wanted to make love.

She refused.

Understanding what she needed from the male to keep her mind sharp, even acquiescing to the act, was one thing. But she would not lay with Sovereign as she had sometimes lain with Que.

If she had to mate him, then they would fuck. Period.

By the time Sovereign came roaring, she had bitten him, torn off pieces, left marks across his neck from the powerful squeeze of her grip around his throat. As always, Sovereign had brought her body to a point that climax made her vision go blank. She'd lay panting, sated and pleased, and let him pet her when she was too scattered to scratch or claw anymore. He'd kiss each wound their play had inspired, tease his tongue in her mouth until she was drunk on him, and if he was clever, slip his cock back into her body to ride her as a lover rode what he adored.

The claws would return as soon as her pleasure began to crest. Restraining her was the only way to take her gently. Even so, he could only manage a few minutes.

"Karhl longs to return to you, Sigil. You enjoyed his touch." Warm words Sovereign cooed at her ear. "We could share you again."

So it was bribery today?

Knowing her resistance to soft touches aggravated the Emperor only brought Sigil more joy in denying them. Furthermore, Sovereign wanted the Lord Commander there to further his own agenda, she was sure of it. No answer was given, only a groan when clever fingers pinched down each bone in her spine.

"He personally stands guard at the gate to this wing, has not slept in his vigil—allows none to enter or disturb your peace, though some have tried."

Voice hoarse, Sigil refuted, "Dryden enters. The women enter."

"They have never left, Sigil. They keep to their rooms when not in use to you. Only I enter and exit that gate."

The all-important High Adherent was locked in with her? The concept seemed a bit ridiculous. Sovereign caught the twitch at the corner of her mouth, and gave it a lingering kiss. "Why do you dislike the Adherents?"

"I dislike you all."

With a smug smile in his voice, Sovereign disagreed, "That is not true, beloved."

His touch on her spine ended, the male rolling them until the mattress was at her back. Eyes holding hers, he waited for an answer. Instead, Sigil chose a subject that made no sense, that pestered her thinking. "On the hologram, Corths holds Jerla's hand. Does he do so because he knows I'm watching?"

Sovereign seemed to consider, lightly pursing his lips while projecting no negative emotion. "Corths is unusual. Though stronger than any human, he is physically inferior to his Brothers. Had he not been only a child when the Alliance fell, he would have died in battle. His strength lies in an intellect both creative and brilliant. He is one of the greatest medical minds in our galaxy." Three awkward words summed it up. "He is soft."

Weakness did not advance one through the ranks of the Brotherhood. "Yet he claims a high rank."

Scoffing, Sovereign nuzzled her cheek. "Did you imagine I would leave you in the care of an unworthy Brother for forty-seven years?"

The tension left her limbs, Sigil went lax. Pinching the bridge of her nose, she kept her eyes shut. Face in a grimace, she longed to scrub her eyes with the meat of her palm, to roll onto her belly and hide in her pillow. "I want—"

Enthusiastic fervor came too eager in Sovereign's voice. "What do you want?"

The obvious answers—freedom, Jerla, the death of the Empire—seemed too simple. Like a rope pulled overly tight, the fibers holding Sigil together had begun to snap. The cord frayed, and a fragmented girl looked into eyes like the ocean.

Impulse moved her. Sigil's lips crashed into the surprised, parted mouth of a thrilled man, her hand cupped his cheek, and she earned her designation.

She struck without thinking.

A crack, a wheeze of breath, and Sovereign lay under her, his neck broken. Eyes rolling in their sockets to find her, the Emperor took in her confusion. How she'd manage it, he was not entirely certain. How she seemed to hover, to lay his body in a position that might increase comfort, bizarre.

Pulling at her hair, Sigil sat on her haunches and stared down at the strongest of the Brotherhood laid out before her. It was hard for her to breathe, though not as hard as it was for him. Sovereign's spinal cord, though not severed, was severely compressed.

He couldn't move.

He couldn't speak, lips parting like a fish out of water.

She could kill him at that very moment… and she wanted to—longed for it greatly.

"It would be so easy…" Her voice, the grain to it, sounded nothing like her. Tears fell down reddened cheeks to behold such a sight, the little rivers rubbed away by the back of her hand. "Fuck me all you like, you cannot change what I am."

Icy eyes darted to the invisible door between her and the terrace, the one she could not open, though she'd tried in passing when watchful eyes might not notice. Sovereign was the key. Thoughts of gnawing through his wrist, of taking his hand for a trophy, were quickly abandoned, for Sigil did not know how long she had before the call to arms was made.

She hefted his dead weight, lifted the Emperor's limp arm, and heard the hiss of the lock decompressing when it was waved before the wall. Laying him carefully down, smoothing back tousled dark hair, she left Sovereign with a view of the broken sky over Irdesi Prime and leapt naked from the balcony and into the dark.

Chapter 8

During another burst of short-lived rain, Sigil found cover beneath a sand-colored awning. At her back, the air was warm and smelled of freshly baked bread. But it was not the rain, or hunger, that drove her there. It was a mind almost as vacant of emotion as Que's—serene—amidst a flock buzzing in a tune that aggravated her mind. In that small shop, she found a woman who appeared somewhere between young and old, almost ageless despite the light creases proving time marched on.

Leaning against the wall, arms casually crossed over the brown, stolen raiment of the lowest caste, Sigil watched the woman hum and knead dough.

She felt unharried, oddly comfortable.

After walking much of the city, merging with the pilgrims who moved from holy site to holy site, her bones were tired, her dread disconnected, and a moment's quiet the most precious commodity she might steal.

The city was beyond her.

A place like Irdesi should not exist, let alone serve as the seat of Imperial power. Hours searching and Sigil had found no ships, no cruisers, no modern transportation in the capital. Converts moved by ancient means—walking until one's legs ached, carrying burdens on their backs through the city's avenues. Stranger still were the hover-carts pulled by four-legged animals that stank and shit in the street.

Life was lived as if all collected were primitives. Even the woman was *making* bread when machines could produce food in seconds.

"You may come inside." The baker's voice matched the mind, calm and even.

Sigil's attention left the crowd to make cruel eyes at the baker. "I have no currency."

Freckled cheeks fattened into a smile, left the woman beautiful. "There is a bench there. Sit."

The bench in question was worn smooth from use, carved of wood, and most certainly from off-world. A swish of dirty robes, and Sigil obeyed, adjusting the hood concealing bright hair and the unnatural vibrancy of her eyes. "Am I to thank you?"

"You're new to pilgrimage, I see."

Lying seemed best. "I am."

The woman's eyes went back to dough braided between precise fingers. "The sensation—assimilation discomfort—will pass."

Humans were no more assimilated than a swarm of mosquitos. "And what makes you so wise? You must have been born here?"

Unworried, a temperate answer was offered. "No. I was purified on Gvtiin IV."

Shoulder blades pressed against the bakery's walls, Sigil gripping her cloak tight around her. "And your family?"

"My family lacked the strength to surmount Conversion." No trace of sadness echoed from the woman with flour embedded under her fingernails. She even had the audacity to gently smile.

"I lost my family too." Quinn had lost her mother, her friend… Taking her eyes from the cracked tile floor to once again view the woman making bread, Sigil muttered, "But not to Conversion."

A dark hand lifted a fresh bun from the pile at the baker's elbow. "Here."

Gifts were never freely given, of that Sigil was certain. "What do you want for it?"

"Your opinion." The smile in her words lightened the air. "This is a new recipe I was hoping to take in offering to the palace. Do you like it?"

It smelled good, sat warm in Sigil's grip when she snatched at the treat. One taste was better than all the confections piled high by the Brotherhood up in their citadel. But when Sigil swallowed, the dough sat thick in her throat. Her eyes watered. "I like it."

Sagely, the baker filled an earthenware cup with water and left it on the counter where her guest might reach. "Where are you from?"

Sigil was unsure what an honest answer to that question might be. Condor? The lonely planet where she'd hunted humans for food? Que's ship? Pax? "I was born on a moon hovering over an enemy world very different from this place. I never liked it there."

"I can't blame you for that. Sounds like the stage for a great deal of discord."

Smarter words no human had ever spoken. Looking to the cup, Sigil took it. The water had a mineral taste, another bite of bread a hint at honey, both softening Sigil's next words. "I have never seen a living being create bread."

"Simplicity is the key to bliss." Rounded shoulders shrugged, the woman winking as if her words had been a gentle jest. "It's an art form, I think, to work with one's hands."

Maybe that was why the people in the strange human city seemed to prefer an antiquated lifestyle. "I used to dance" —Sigil found it hard to say aloud— "before Sovereign came. I think I understand what you mean. Now I have nothing… to do."

But there were always things the Brotherhood wanted her to do, not one moment of their schedule interesting in any way.

"We all have our place." The baker reached for another lump of dough. "That is the beauty of our society. If you cannot find yours, the Adherents will assign you a role that suits the needs of the collective. Enriching the whole will enrich you."

The idea was not appealing. "Did they order you to make bread?"

"No. I was originally tasked to supply and clean a warship's galley. In my work, I discovered a talent for enhancing soldier's provisions with things collected from various stations and planets we passed. When my service contract was up for review, Admiral Gethman approved my request for access to

Irdesi Prime. Transfer was granted. Now I make bread; I have a shop.”

Mention of a Brother chipped her calm, Sigil confounded that even something as insignificant as a woman making bread had been hand selected. “You were placed here as if part of the scenery. A puzzle piece. The Emperor wants the city this way…”

“This is holy ground; care must be taken in who is allowed to cultivate it.”

The conversation could not have been more foreign to Sigil. “I saw many *holy sites* today—tombs, statues from other worlds, monuments to battles, even the water that runs down the mountain you call holy.”

Brown eyes sparkling, the baker asked, “Did you see the Adherents’ Cathedral?”

“No.” And Sigil had no plan on approaching anywhere near it.

“The Emperor’s lady has awoken. We live at a time in our empire when the miraculous has begun. Celebrations like Irdesi has never seen clog the square before it. I’ll sell my bread there later, and if I am lucky, tonight she’ll show herself to us.”

The joy in the stranger’s voice lessened the baker in Sigil’s eyes. “I understand she is reluctant to bear that title.”

Humming as if she too had heard such a rumor, the baker said, “Humility is her greatest attribute. The Consort’s example shames those who try to reach too far.”

Here was Sigil's chance to see what effect a taboo word might have. "Like the Soshiia?"

Spitting on the floor, the baker lost the internal peace which had attracted Sigil in the first place. "Unsalvageable are a taint she has already begun to flush out. The Imperial Consort will cleanse the ranks of those who refuse all which our lady's suffering has given us."

Face emotionless, Sigil stared. "And you will make bread."

"And one day my offering may sit on her table."

The amount of food left ignored each day on that long, black table—how much of it had been made by the hands of people who revered a monster? "It was kind of you to give me something you intended for her."

The baker's smile returned, as did her tranquility. "She would not want one of her people to go hungry."

All her life, Sigil had walked through suffering masses and had little interest in those around her. She was nothing like what this woman described. "And the Emperor?" The one Sigil had left hardly breathing. "What of him?"

"Incorruptible."

A bit of water caught in Sigil's throat, a cough—almost a laugh. "Next you'll profess that Tessans don't strangle their yellow hatchlings at birth, claiming golden scales denote a child who will be mentally unstable and dangerous to itself and others."

Lips curved, white teeth on display. "Have you ever seen a yellow scaled Tessan?"

"No."

"I have." Dirty hood hiding the majority of her expression, Sigil cooed, "Their genocide is not due to mental instability. The Tessan Authority has them secretly murdered because yellow scaled males possess the same prowess as their superlative female counterparts."

"I know nothing of these things." Another smile, apple-cheeked and glowing. "My concerns hardly extend beyond the making of bread."

Too much time Sigil had spent in one place.

Standing, she sighed, "And that, lamb, is why you are happy and I am in misery."

Sigil left the kind baker alive, a decision regretted almost immediately when Imperial soldiers grew thick on the terrace mileage she was confined to.

Enough time had passed. Sovereign had healed, his anger roused. When they found her, he would punish her…

He would lock her away in a jail even darker than the city under its clouds and rain.

And this place—this kingdom—was where Converts aspired to be? So they might be some part of a commune specially selected to what? Impress her? Where their dwellings lacked the gaudy opulence in *her* palace prison? A beacon in the human universe.

What of the sumptuousness on the top of the mountain? What of the Great Houses lurking at court and married to Sovereign's Brothers? Sigil had not seen them, but she knew what waited in those halls.

Irdesi Prime was nothing more than one big stage.

The moon, Condor, was the only real thing about this place, looming as it did over palace and city alike—the former seat of Alliance military innovation. That was reality hanging fat and ugly on the other side of an angry atmosphere.

Sovereign had been born there.

Sigil had been born there.

They may have even shared the same womb.

Maybe that was why her eyes darted up, hungry for a sight of it. Maybe that was why she wanted to reach past the clouds and crush that unseen spherical mass, so lies that led to happy, simple bakers might keep.

If this place was how life churned on in the Empire, it was nothing like any life she'd known. The humans, every soul around her, had been something else before the Imperium smashed down on their existence. And now they were happy? The Unsalvageable made more sense, seemed more honorable. At least they fought back.

And what would Unsalvageable cities look like?

Probably like Pax.

The thought made her homesick even as it turned her stomach. Overthinking, paying little attention, Sigil bumped into the man walking before her. He stopped, and it wasn't only him. All around her humans paused in their strides, standing still, and looking up at the sky.

Ready to bolt, assuming she'd been found, Sigil felt it before the sound registered. Rich, melodious noise crawled up the soles of her feet, through bone, over skin, saturating every cell until she vibrated in time with that note.

Sigil's world became quiet, like the mind of the abandoned baker.

There was no pain.

She felt no sorrow.

And that harmony, it came from all the humans pressed about her, beyond her, filling the city to stare up, just as the sky fractured into a beauty of prismatic light. Jaw agape, she too stared into the cracked canopy, into the flashes breaking up the dark as if frayed pieces sought out their broken ends. For the briefest moment, Sigil felt whole.

She belonged, felt connected to everything around her.

The sensation was alien, exotic, outlandish—like a memory of her mother singing in her thoughts.

That sound, that balm, ended too soon, leaving her gasping for air.

The sheep around her began to move, each Convert continuing their path as if no interruption had taken place. The stranger at her side said nothing about how she'd gripped his hand and unconsciously threaded their fingers together. He just let her go, so he too might move on.

Frightened, backing away, Sigil sought refuge from the crowd in the first open door she found—a tavern, empty but for a few Converts wandering back to their seats after the song outside. Sigil sat, ordered a pitcher of spirits, and swallowed the first cup so greedily the knot in her throat was forced to relax.

And then he sat, taking the bench across from her, grinning meanly.

As she had failed to find an escape, it was inevitable one would find her. He'd probably tracked her all day, laughing from shadows when she didn't notice how close he really was.

Lowering the cup from her lips, Sigil wiped the back of her hand over her mouth and admitted recognition. "I've wondered why I hadn't been forced to look at your ugly face yet."

Settling his armored mass, smirking as if everything he saw before him could not be more droll, Lord Commander Tiburon asked, "And just what do you think you're doing?"

"Exploring." The fizzy drink went back to her lips, the clay cup hiding her answer. "This is the capital after all—the seat of the Empire."

The Lord Commander sat quietly, watching her, that unshakable smirk delighted. When her gaze slipped over the metal-filled scar running across his face, he audibly purred. Waiting for her attention to slip back to his eyes, waiting for Sigil to see the brilliant green so she might remember it was his eye she'd swallowed first, Tiburon took the waiting pitcher and filled a cup for himself. "You look exactly as I expected you would. Pathetic."

"You look the same."

His finger traced the tip of the scar. "More or less."

Sigil breathed, "You were ugly before I tore open your face."

"Brat." A dry laugh stressed that the room had grown utterly silent, every human having left on some unseen order. "You really are impossible to please. It's fucking entertaining watching them try though."

The thought had crossed her mind once or twice.

Bracing for calamity, Sigil asked, "How long until Sovereign shows up to drag me back?"

"That implant wired through your brain," Tiburon cocked his chin, eyeing her forehead. "I was the one who demanded the Brotherhood mesh a tracker into the circuitry. Sovereign refused, claiming the risk was too great should your enemies harness technology that could trace you… And you do have enemies, Sigil." He took a long drink, a drip spilling down a strong chin. "My point is this. Sovereign doesn't know you're here. Subsequently, he doesn't know I'm with you. Take advantage of that."

Sigil leaned nearer. "And why, of all your bastard Brothers, do you think I would believe a word that comes from your mouth? I've read Arden's histories… they are full of your lies."

"That's not to say Sovereign won't descend eventually." Tiburon rolled several slender vials across the table, their contents a familiar murky white.

If they were what she suspected, Sigil found them almost as disgusting as she found them valuable.

The Lord Commander smiled, two teeth chipped, marring his beauty even as the metal scar enhanced it. "I offer you time. If you're wise, you will take it."

Sigil snatched at the semen-filled vials to stuff them into her cloak. "Why?"

A parcel was tossed to plop before her. "And there you have currency. You can run free, brat. Walk the surface of the planet, take in the sights."

Pulling the coarse sack to her breast, Sigil's eyes went wide, her psionics snapping as she waited for the trap to spring and crush the spark of hope in her ribs. "You think I'll tell him the truth? Is that why you do this?"

Amusement bent the scar, twisted Tiburon's lips. He refilled her glass. "Tell Sovereign what you will. Tell him how we stood face to face on Condor, and how I told you the path necessary to escape the compound. Tell him I have hunted you, found you, and how you ripped my face apart when I last had you pinned to the floor. Tell him how you let me live after gorging on my eye and tongue. Tell him that afterward you rubbed yourself against me until you orgasmed.”

Unsure, Sigil ran her finger over the rim of her cup. “You were already in the room where they kept my mother. The human doctor I’m remembered for murdering, you killed.”

“The human? You would call *that* human? Dr. Saniel was your architect, Sigil—my creator, your creator. Every piece of you was chosen to glorify her, you even vaguely bear a resemblance. And there you stood all those years ago, crying over a limbless, alien lump you called mommy while the nearest genetic relation you ever truly had screamed for you to save her from me.”

A scream Sigil had ignored. “You slaughtered that human.”

“I did.”

“And told the Brotherhood I was the one responsible for the death of the scientist who designed and implemented Project Cataclysm.”

“True.”

Watching that face, the clean cut of his jaw, the shaved smoothness of Tiburon’s skull, Sigil demanded. “Why?”

“Every last one of us subsists on lies. The Brotherhood glorifies fables. You heard your own today, *magnanimous saint of the people*. So I offer you this; I will always tell you the truth. They won’t. Sovereign lies to you. Karhl lies. Arden lies. They lie to each other.”

"And you lie to them." Just like his Brothers, he had not answered her question, simply shifted conversation to enhance his agenda. She asked again, "Why did you tell them I murdered Dr. Saniel?"

Lord Commander Tiburon shrugged. "Because I wanted to. Your madness on Condor gave me a perfect opportunity to further my interests. Her death I found *very* interesting."

"Did you know her?" Sigil's only interaction with the doctor had been purely clinical—tests, torture, the resetting of limbs.

When his smile disappeared, Tiburon seemed far more dangerous than even Sovereign. "I knew her."

The door was fifty paces to her right, a window twenty paces to the left. All those measurements taken without Sigil moving her gaze from those moss green eyes. "There are things you want to tell me, Brotherhood lies. What are they?"

Head cocking, Tiburon frowned. He watched her. He calculated. "It doesn't work that way, brat. I can't read your mind and we don't have all night. You must ask specific questions. Or do you anticipate I will throw the right answers at your feet, as I have tossed you money and my ejaculate?"

Frustrated with a man who was obviously playing with her, Sigil hissed, "Who are the Soshiia?"

By the way Tiburon leaned back into his chair, Sigil had obviously asked the right question. "Karhl is the oldest of us—a century older than I. The fact he still lives is testament to his unprecedented design. He's all that's left of the original batch. And there have been others who failed, who lacked perfection, who died in service—each of us ultimately replaceable… until I disemboweled our creator" — His face, his beauty grew ruined with a hateful snarl— "and crushed her brilliant brain to mush. The expertise in grafting whatever it is we are was lost that day. We cannot be recreated."

The Brotherhood would have cloned her had they been able to… that is what his words implied. She would have been free, worthless. His actions made her life necessary to the group. "The Soshiia are… more of you… outside your Brotherhood? Soldiers who absconded before the Alliance fell?"

At once Tiburon's nasty mask snapped back. "They could be. Considering that the Soshiia are capable of overcoming the biological alterations of Conversion by replacing it with something else… considering their training and resistance to interrogation. Who taught them? Who meddled with their chemistry? Maybe they are pawns of faulty Brothers who seek to slither in and steal what is not theirs. Maybe they are something else."

It could not be possible. "Was there another Sovereign? One that led before this one?"

One eyebrow cocked. "Once, I was Sovereign."

And Karhl was the oldest...

"How many?"

"Seven." As if disappointed by her indifferent reaction, Tiburon changed the subject. "Why have you not asked me how many children were bred from your sleeping body?"

It caught in her throat, that first eruption of beer fizzed vomit she choked down. The possibility Sovereign had committed such a horrible act was one she'd not allowed herself to consider. Hearing such an atrocity spoken aloud sent her instantly past caution.

Had her psionics been unhindered by whatever mess those bastards had jammed into her brain, the entirety of that lounge would have been blasted apart. Instead, all the furnishings rose and trembled, her cup shattering in her grip.

"Don't tell me you didn't suspect?" False pity shown on Tiburon's face. He pouted his lips. "Almost fifty years you slept, suffering brain damage that required more surgeries than I can count, and you woke in a state of psychosis. Did you really expect Sovereign could respect your… womb? An entire species depends on your genetics."

In a fury, she launched herself across the table. Raking her nails over Tiburon's throat, biting him until she tasted blood—all she did only roused laughter. The Brother who had come close to catching her so many times, she knew his face, his scent, the workings of his mind, and shattered his nose… and still he laughed.

In her rage, Sigil did not see Tiburon's strike, but she felt her cheek break, the flesh of her lip split.

They stilled, Sigil crouched over the smiling snake.

In a shaky breath, she demanded, "How many daughters have the Brotherhood stolen from me?"

Under her, the bloodied man offered another truth. "None. While you slept, your body refused to ovulate, and the circuitry of your reproductive organs is too *alien* to be manipulated safely. If we were to inadvertently damage you—"

Snarling, she gripped Tiburon's throat. "But it was attempted."

"No." Shoving away the nonplused woman, Tiburon scowled and stood. "You should know your Jerla woke this morning. He asks for you." Sigil made no move to rise, crouched at the feet of a madman who knew just how to mindfuck her. The Lord Commander sighed. "There is no exit from this planet. No ships, brat. The best you can do is hide. Maybe pass your hours *baking bread*." His eyes went to a vial of semen dropped amidst their skirmish, his toe kicked it toward her. "I have given you the means to be left alone. Use the opportunity to *reason* like an adult. Your tantrums bore me. Gratitude for my effort would be appropriate."

Gratitude? Face red, jaw swollen, she glared at the armored warrior. "And the price for this miraculous *help*?"

That cruel smile snapped back to pretty lips. He reached out to ghost a touch over her ruined cheek. "Consider it foreplay."

She bit off two of his fingers.

Chapter 9

Fluid-filled vials rattled each time Sigil rolled her palm. Staring down at the sorry collection, her tongue wiggled a loose tooth, the knitting bones of her jaw painful.

Each capped vessel was self-contained, frozen by an unseen power source, and could prove to be ultimately useless—or much more dangerous to the Brotherhood than even Tiburon, intended.

But which was it?

Seven cycles Sovereign claimed she'd endured without his *liquid contribution*. Seven cycles from the time he'd left her on the Water Planet until she'd asked Karhl to deliver her to Irdesi Prime.

Seven was a grand improvement over those first days on Pax—days when one cycle had sent her on a mindless rampage.

But this was Lord Commander Tiberon's sperm, potentially less potent.

Furthermore, he *wanted* her to use it. He wanted it badly.

As he'd claimed, the sack at her shoulder held a great deal of money—enough to see Sigil through for months in the capital.

None of that mattered.

Because he'd also told her Jerla was awake.

Sigil was many things—most of them bad—but when her mind was unconsumed, she was not unintelligent. She'd been designed to be brilliant, possessing neural pathways eons of evolutions beyond that of a human. But even the most simple-minded Convert could see Tiburon wanted the Imperial Consort to run amok. And from what she'd sensed inside him, the Lord Commander believed strongly in what he hoped to inspire in a newly acquired *volatile resource*.

Calculating, having dealt with him in the past, Sigil assumed nothing and questioned everything. Whatever he was up to was not some artless conspiracy—not when it felt as if centuries were folded into Tiburon's doings.

He, unlike his Brothers, was rooted in intention she could not grasp—like what he'd done to Dr. Saniel on Pax. There was a patience in the man, an ancient, crawling endurance, unhurried to render its goal. But Sigil had seen what happened when Tiburon found his moment.

What he'd done to the doctor was beyond even her vicious moments of weakness.

He'd tormented that horrid woman, killed her slowly enough the doctor's nerves appreciated optimal suffering.

Weary of the taste of blood in her mouth, Sigil reached two fingers between her lips. The loose tooth was not going to mend. A new one would have to be grown. Pinching it, she yanked. A squishy hole gaped in her gums. Sigil held up her fingers, the bloody incisor jagged and uninspiring.

Tiburon had hurt her, intentionally inflicted damage with each swing after she'd bit him... so unlike Sovereign. The Emperor was always cautious when they'd tangled. He conquered, he didn't crush. He never broke one of her bones or rent flesh.

But Tiburon... both of them took pleasure in giving the other physical pain. They had fought like cats—scraping and biting—until each grew bored, slinking away to their respective corners to lick bloody wounds. She had enjoyed it. He had enjoyed it—his bliss broadcasted so violently, Sigil had laughed at the familiarity of such raw sensation.

It had been... fun.

He echoed her insides. Had she ripped him open and crawled through his guts, it would have been her own entrails poked, yanked, and savored.

Whether or not Tiburon understood the effect his actions had on her mattered little. What did matter were facts.

Fact One: The Lord Commander had claimed there were no ships, no way off the planet. Sigil believed him. But after a century of escape, she knew one thing to be true above all others. There was always a way out.

Fact Two: Even if she ran, there was nothing but the promise that madness would return no matter how far she fled. Secondly, without Que, what she'd do once possessed by that madness would be terrible.

Fact Three: Que was dead. He wasn't coming back. Ever.

Que was dead. He was dead. He was dead and she was alive. That was not going to change. The money in her sack would not change it. The vials in her grip would not change it. Rampaging through the Convert's capital would do nothing to alter what had come to pass.

Every urge she ached to satisfy would ultimately prove pointless.

Killing puny, little humans who had been chemically mutilated by the Brotherhood seemed… redundant. She could break even the strongest Convert specimen with a flick of the wrist. She could hunt them, play with them, they could even serve as her food.

But how strange Converts were.

Her history with humans had been… uncomfortable. Memory of her long-dead handlers, of the outlaws who'd shot her ship from the sky, a cold reminder that—as a collective—the species was very dangerous. Humans had designed Condor and enabled Dr. Saniel to experiment on sentient beings. Humans had wielded dominion over Project Cataclysm against their own kind. Humans had tortured a little girl so she might be a better killer.

Sovereign believed them to be dangerous. So much so, he had conquered every last feral he could reach, firm in the notion they posed a threat to her. Now, this new breed of Converts was *his* weapon of calculated design.

They sang at the sky when gloomy day became dark night. They baked bread.

Sigil had walked amongst them, watched their dealings, seen them meet in droves anticipating a glimpse of the Imperial Consort. They seemed content with their lot in life.

Of course, this was only an example of one tightly controlled population. Outlying worlds, newly conquered soil, would echo differently.

Or did Conversion wear the same face, only the environment changed?

Sigil didn't know.

Looking at the bloody tooth, at the dirty fingers pinching it, she frowned and tossed the thing away. The vials jingled again, the noise they made similar to the chimes in Karhl's hair.

The thought stilled her hand. The image of tightly veiled pain in his eyes when she'd told him to leave her alone, the echo of disappointment inside him—itching memory came with that sound. The Lord Commander had retreated, he'd stood waiting, guarding the gate into her rooms.

To keep others out, or keep her in?

In a sparse room set aside for those making pilgrimage, Sigil sighed.

Too long she'd been chaff blown about by the Brotherhood's wind—this way and that way, up and down—she'd been flung, stretched, and damaged. It was exhausting. But Sigil didn't have to be so pathetic. She need not be *Sigil* or *Quinn*. She didn't need the vials or Tiburon's money. There was no reason to languish so fools might paint her white and Heralds might seduce with stories and play.

Sovereign stood rigid, glaring upon a population packed before the Adherents' Cathedral. They'd begun to plead up at the viaduct where palace met basilica, calling out for Sigil as if their cry might coax the elusive female to appear.

"Report." The coldness of the order warned further disappointment was not an option.

"I have been unable to find her, Sovereign."

Stormy eyes left the frenzied crowd to burn upon the Brother who disappointed him most. The Emperor said nothing.

Even Arden was unable to conceal the fear that that look inspired. "She is in the city, I am certain of it. It is only a matter of time..."

Tiburon stood nearby, chewing on a hard roll as he watched the exchange.

Sovereign shot his displeasure toward his scarred councilor. "Show him."

There was no movement between the men, but an image projected in their midst. The Herald focused his sole attention on the figure sweeping a floor.

Arden hated all he saw. "Our female stands in rags performing menial labor."

Lord Commander Tiburon grinned. "Is that all you see? Open your eyes, schemer. Sigil is engaging with a human. She talks to this one. She asks questions, returns daily and remains longer."

"Daily?" As if he were Emperor, Arden hissed, "How is it you possess such information yet Sigil is not in our presence?"

Tiburon made no answer, his silence condescension enough.

The Herald's hands tightened until knuckles popped. "Karhl will not support this! You will not have your way!"

Tiburon's smirk became a sneer.

"She smiles." Sovereign's voice cut through the Brothers' squabble. "Right there" —he froze the image—"Sigil is smiling."

It was a shy thing displayed by that flickering hologram, the smallest offering of curved lips, like the creature emoting was unsure how to do it.

As if his joke ended, Lord Commander Tiburon lost all pretense. Grave, he addressed Arden. "A new companion for her has been found. You are no longer required, Herald, and are to be reassigned immediately."

"YOU CANNOT DO THIS!"

"He can, with my sanction." The Emperor barely contained his vast anger under a grim mask. "Three days and you have failed to find her. Yet over those three days one human has had the profound influence on my Sigil, *you* failed to inspire. Your enthusiasm is noteworthy, but your results lackluster.

Be grateful you live and may see her from time to time."

Arden shook in his rage, muscles flexed, jaw ticking. Golden eyes full of hate flashed toward the Lord Commander. "Tiburon doesn't love her. He can't!"

Sovereign had heard enough. "You are dismissed, Arden. Leave."

The Herald marched off, stiff and awkward at the order. What had once been Sovereign's favorite Brother disappeared, swallowed into the dark of the palace. Only the Emperor and the Lord Commander remained. As if there had been no unpleasantness, Sovereign reached out to touch the projection of the woman he pined for, his fingers distorting the hologram. "There is no commendation earned in your actions, Tiburon… I find your practices hardly above Arden's. Continue on this path and I will be forced to act against you."

"The Empire would fall."

"You, of all of us, most understand the concept you are replaceable." Sovereign turned his back on the deadly soldier. "Remember that. And remember that I love her."

Sanctimonious, Tiburon purred, "No. You don't."

Days watching and it was the same. The children, they ran through the streets—fearless. They played outside, unmonitored. Loud. Sigil could not help but stare. Her eyes tracing a girl kicking a ball, Sigil spoke to the baker working at the table behind her. "I like it here. You're quiet."

Light laughter came with no comment.

As Sigil was always asking questions and demanding answers, silence never lasted long in the bakery.

Turning to the Convert, Sigil tapped her fingertip against her skull and explained. "You misunderstand. You're quiet here." Her attention went back to the street. "Everyone else makes so much noise. Always something, something they want: hunger, greed, sadness, lust, guilt, thirst, pain—each *something* pointless in a place like this—a place where you have everything. But then there's you. You're… quiet."

"And that is why you come here each day?"

"Yes." Trying to invoke human politeness, Sigil added the baker's name, a name she'd purposefully asked for so the human might recognize she held interest, "Elba."

Elba nodded at the nonsense and wisely remained *silent*.

Sigil slipped toward the bench. "I want you to take me to the Adherents' Cathedral. If you will do so, I will help you sell your bread in the square this evening." The offer was a generous one… considering.

The baker stopped fiddling with her dough. She wiped her hands on the sackcloth at her waist. "This is not an evening for selling bread in the square. Condor is visible. Few will gather past *the fracturing*. It's a night for reflection and seclusion."

Too late to stop her hiss, Sigil lost a touch of control. "And what is Condor to you?"

The baker's answer was immediate, memorized, "A remnant of pain, of loss, even Conversion cannot wash away."

Adjusting her hood, Sigil looked for the words required to get her way. "Am I to say please?"

"You are frustrated." Elba took a seat at Sigil's side. "Yet I didn't say no. I only claimed it was not a good night to sell bread."

"So you will escort me to the cathedral? You will tell me, in your words, not in Adherents' preaching, why it matters."

The woman nodded, her dark skin slightly greyed by a day's dusting of flour.

"Can we go now?"

Few mustered on terraces, streets, or public areas, just as the baker warned. That was as much a blessing as a curse. The change in atmosphere altered the weather. The typical crispness sat instead like cold sweat on the skin. Fabric clung.

The effect was obvious on shivering Elba. Sigil was unaffected as they stood near enough the cathedral to view the gates. It stuck from elevation, like a broken bone jutting through flesh. Unlike the other earth shaded buildings on Irdesi, unlike even the mountainside palace, the cathedral was white. The Adherents' Cathedral stood as focal point of the capital, with its turrets and blazing colorlessness.

Sigil had seen it from afar. She knew it was markedly different, but approaching such a monolith in person was uncanny.

Banked on either side of the Adherents' seat of power stood two figures, each stone warden facing the other. Like warring kings. On the left rose Tiburon, formidable and frowning in his armor—to the right Karhl, his statue far less welcoming. Almost as tall as the pale edifice itself, they acted sentinel, dwarfing all brave enough to pass between the Empire's titans.

Considering the citizen's disquiet with Condor's rising, a great many citizens and pilgrims alike lingered on the sprawling steps that reached down to every level. The closer Sigil approached, the more she found the minds around her took in that building in the opposite sentiment.

Standing on white steps brought them comfort, gave them succor.

In the cathedral's shadow there was a tone to what she sensed: love—the real kind.

The kind Jerla's mother never had for her yellow-scaled offspring.

Sigil glanced at the profile of the guide projecting such a feeling.

Elba smiled in the way that made her face pleasing.

Unsure what her companion found so splendid, Sigil sought clarification, "Tell me of the gates."

"Lord Commander Tiburon spearheaded the campaign against my world, killed our royals himself. He delivered me, offered purpose and compassion. Across from him stands the figure of Lord Commander Karhl. He does not exist to forgive. He exists to cleanse the soul. Worlds under his thumb shall be swept barren, ready for devoted Converts to populate."

Sigil frowned. "That is common sentiment… admiration for those who ruined worlds?"

"Should it be different?"

Was that why Karhl had been brought to Pax? To cleanse it? Was the white-haired warrior who'd tried so hard all those years ago to be gentle with her only waiting to hand her off and kill all the lifeforms Sigil had slaughtered in her rage? "Karhl was amongst those sent to my home." There would be some reaction at her words, Sigil was sure of it. "I had heard rumor of him, terrible things. Seeing him again, was unsettling."

A thick brow rose. "Again?"

"I first saw him when I was only a child."

Elba's oval chin pointed to the cathedral gates. "Perhaps that is why you were chosen for pilgrimage?"

And that was another thing Sigil had come to learn from the baker. Not all pilgrims came to walk the path seeking absolution and power out of choice; some were *chosen* by governing Adherents. Imperial law—the compulsion of Conversion—made the honor one that could not be willingly refused.

Elba saw Sigil hesitate, took her hand and guided her up the steps. Together they passed high ranked Imperial retainers, elite soldiers, the dregs of the lowest pilgrim… no less than three Brothers.

"Successful pilgrimage will raise your rank. If you exceed expectation, you may even be allowed to make your home here." Elba met her eye and drew her past the sentinels. "We could talk more often."

The doors, though tall, let in very little sun. Scant light sliced in, illuminating a single stone figure and forcing the eye right to it. Atop a pedestal, stood a little girl holding a basin in fragile hands, her slow dripping tears caught to pool within the platter.

It was Sigil.

Seeing the stone figure hollowed out her breath, it stopped her feet. That statue was a lie. Never. Never in her childhood had Sigil been so undamaged. Yet the rendered girl showed no obvious broken bones, no weekly disfigurement. The sad face was carved to be unbruised, even pretty.

"The Imperial Consort as a child." Elba dipped her fingertip into the basin, as did others who passed by. A single captured drop of fluid, was put on her tongue. The baker swallowed.

Sigil mimicked the action. She dipped her finger set it between her lips.

It did not taste of tears. It did not taste of water.

Seeing the stony reaction on the face of her guest, Elba explained, "The serum of Conversion. Her gift to us, so all humanity might be joined and transformed."

Looking at that bowl, at more and more visitors dipping their fingers in to collect their droplet, Sigil whispered. "I had a doll once, something worn… old."

"My mother carved my toys," Elba spoke, the memory of a woman who was most likely murdered by the Empire remembered with no bitterness, no fuel for revenge, only fond feeling.

It bothered Sigil for a human to speak as if they shared a special memory, to lack wrath for the dead. "No, woman, you see... I had the doll for less than a cycle." Unable to peel her eyes from the stone girl, Sigil reached out to touch the lie. The statue was warm, the ripples of its carved rags seemingly soft. The exact opposite of her chilling voice. "They had to saw off my hands to take it away. When I was *persuaded* to kill the woman who gave me the gift, I did so with only my teeth. She screamed a great deal, though mostly from what was done to her before I was thrown into the room. That's the only time I recall childhood weeping that was not inspired by an involuntary reaction to torture." And that had to have been why Sovereign had thought to mention the painful moment on Pax. "I could not have held your shiny basin, and my tears were not an offering for you."

Elba heard Sigil's growled litany, looking both alarmed and bellicose. It was quite an alteration in the baker's natural cool.

The woman prepared to take a step back, to summon Adherents who could correct the problem or remove the female who just might bear the corruption of an Unsalvageable.

Elba's escape was immediately prevented when an iron grip on her arm yanked her nearer. A grimy hood blocked the view of her face, but not the firm set of Sigil's lips as she warned, "You are not to leave. We have not yet finished."

The quiet inside Elba was quiet no more.

As if pulling an errant child, Sigil dragged the captive baker forward. More white stone marked the ground, a backdrop for slithering mosaics—some in muted colors, others in stark reds—branching as if those who understood what they saw could grasp the proper paths. Through the pious, past countless statues depicting Sovereign's brothers, they traveled deeper into the vast *sanctuary*. Wood smoke, incense, a sound similar to the soothing hum shared when the sky of Irdesi Prime fractured, grew overbearing and changed the air.

It affected Sigil; she gripped her captive with an arm around Elba's shoulders, not sure if she herself sought support or needed a greater hold to control. Converts, human-Adherents, shuffled about in their caps and robes, they soliloquized on the Empire and the greatness it inspired in the hearts of mere men and women. They chanted. Where the floor's mosaic was widest, the trunk of the proverbial tree—a pool, small but seemingly serene, lapped. Most who entered gathered there. When pilgrims were offered their chance to kneel and drink—to take clear, pretty poison into their mouths—many fell and died in moments. Few lasted long enough to be collected so they might attain Higher Conversion under the watchful eye of the Adherents.

That's why pilgrims came to Irdesi. It wasn't to see monuments—not unless the sight of such tributes was to inspire strength in their time of trial— it was to offer themselves so they might rise above the low rank all common Converts seemed reborn to. Or be conveniently disposed of.

Mosaics branched. Sigil chose the path the led furthest into the massive chamber. There was more to be seen—it seemed she'd chosen the way for pilgrims to glorify themselves as warriors.

A carved fixture of Karhl, another of Tiburon, one for each of the Empire's five admirals, all possessing either a cup, a bowl, or an upturned, open mouth. Inside the hollows still fluid waited so pilgrims might collect a portion and drink.

Sigil beheld three soldiers swallow the liquid dripping from Tiburon's open jaw. Sigil watched three pilgrims die.

This was how the elites were chosen. This is how hybrids were made.

Sigil looked down at Elba. "I see no basin for Sovereign, only his Brothers."

What had been warm chocolate eyes seemed pitch black in such low light. Glassy and committed, they stared up at her captor, as if Elba suspected something that could not be true.

The baker swallowed and nodded. "Every male statue in this temple depicts a Convert who survived Sovereign's serum. To swallow one so powerful is sure death. Therefore, one must be invited to drink of it. No soul has been granted the opportunity in over a century."

So that was how the seemingly immortal Brotherhood was explained and accepted? It was clever, even brought the tiniest tick to the corner of Sigil's mouth. "And what made Sovereign so powerful?"

Elba was breathless. "The Imperial Consort blessed him long ago."

Sigil could not help but mock the idea. "Then why is she not Empress?"

The question precipitated a programed response. "Our Emperor was born to hold the position in service to her. Her place is not at the head of government. It would distract from her greater purpose—enriching our hearts and unifying our species."

"By crying into a basin?"

Elba stuttered, "We… we all carry a piece of her inside us. She... salvaged us from the mire."

Enough religious babble. Sigil had a purpose. "You have not noticed, baker, but many of the men carved in stone, their living likeness' have arrived." She held the mystified woman nearer, Sigil's lips going to Elba's ear. "Behind me Karhl, behind you Tiburon. Sovereign stands in the middle of that patch of dark. He is watching us right now."

Elba was shaking. "You never use their proper titles when speaking their sacred names."

Ignoring the woman's muttering, Sigil took Elba's wrist. "I need you to bear witness. You are not to leave my side." Sigil entwined their fingers, her whisper edging on desperate, "You are not to speak. Be *quiet*… calm for me… and you will have my gratitude. When this is over, for one evening, I will help you sell your bread."

At Sigil's harshly whispered words, Elba nodded.

The sound of Karhl's hair preceded his approach from her back, Sigil analyzing Tiburon's advance from the opposite direction. Both the giant and scarred one stopped at a reasonable distance, only observing, yet armed and armored.

Shoulder to shoulder with her guest, Sigil poured her attention upon the third male. "The baker is not to be meddled with."

Ignoring the human at her side, Sovereign's fingers caught Sigil's hood, pulling it back so icy eyes were no longer shielded from his view.

"Beloved." The calm, steady voice expressed no anger, no frustration. "Why would I harm a Devout? She has been nothing but exemplary in her behavior."

It was not the time to argue the semantics between the words *meddled with* and *harmed*. Sigil had more pressing matters to address. "I knew you would come if I entered this place." In that flickering light, the planes of his face, the edges of Sovereign's cheeks, seemed carved like the stone men surrounding them. "I thought we might engage in a new experience and… talk."

One corner of Sovereign's mouth rose. He seemed entranced, emotions content. "I enjoy talking with you."

He spoke so gently, she grew frustrated. "I do not want to live in your palace. I cannot… it's too loud. There is too much."

"It wasn't premeditated, not for all your threats. It wasn't your fault." Sovereign's whisper came urgent. "You know I know that."

"I am unhappy there, Sovereign." And she looked vulnerable in that moment, openly admitting weakness.

The Emperor seemed surprised at her words, at the melancholy creasing on her brow. He reached to cup her cheek, fully aware she did not flinch or draw away as she usually did. "No one keeps you in your rooms, beloved. You could have left at any time."

"Don't they? Would I be free to wander alone if I wished? No, there is always a handler, protocol. You have recreated the conditions of Condor."

Pain lanced Sovereign's whisper, a look of longing mirroring the internal burn of those words. "Please… you cannot mean that."

Sigil's brows fell, her eyes pleaded. "Understand that I know this is forever. On a ship, how far would I get before all this *progress* came undone? What would happen without a guardian willing to do whatever was necessary to subdue what I became? Am I to enslave one of you—someone easy to overwhelm physically and turn into him what you would make me—a kept thing used to satiate urges? How long, how far could I run?" Her grip left the fingers of the baker, Sigil fisting the fabric of Sovereign's sleeve. "The knowledge is prison enough. I cannot leave you. This. Is. My. Life."

"You're saying you would not run?"

Sigil's eye ticked. "Find a Kilactarin empath to confirm my honesty, if you must."

"Sigil, beloved, this must stop."

She knew he alluded to the savage guilt that ate her up. She knew he wanted her to view her imprisonment differently. "I know."

"Do you?" Sovereign did not seem so sure. Fingering her hair, closing in on his female, he pressed warm lips to her furrowed forehead.

Allowing him the intimacy, Sigil whispered, "I slept for so long, worlds are beyond my memory. I know nothing of the universe now… I hardly understand the Empire. Reading of your history irritates me. I cannot help it."

"And you've been bored." Sovereign pulled away just far enough to see her eyes flame *can you blame me?* It seemed Sovereign was not so indifferent to her request. "Then let us negotiate. Send off your Convert and we will continue to *talk*, like you wished."

Sigil turned her head, felt Sovereign breathe in the scent of her hair, and looked to the nonplused baker witnessing an exchange that would change the Empire forever. "I thank you for the bread." There was a moment's hesitation before Sigil added, "You're unusual, worthy of the *holy ground* you love. Having walked it, I'm not sure if it's worthy of you."

Elba did not move, the baker looking to Sovereign as if the conversation was one she could not fully comprehend. Addressing Sigil, the woman seemed unsure, "Imperial Consort, *do you wish me to stay?*"

She couldn't help it, Sigil smiled. "I'd prefer it if you called me Quinn."

Tiburon was the one to move—almost too fast for human eyes to follow—to snag the arm of the Convert and whisk her toward the door.

"Quinn?" Sovereign asked, cheeks hollowed as if the name tasted bitter.

"In the city I can be lowly Quinn, pilgrim. If you don't let me get away from Sigil, I'll go insane, implant or no." That was how it had to be so she might maintain this new level of calm. "I want to keep my residence near the bakery. You're not welcome there."

By his emotions, by his expression, such a thought was inconsiderable. "Those pilgrims' dwellings, beloved, are not intended for extended use."

Of course he'd known where she'd been.

Her throat grew hot, Sigil looking for words than might be sung as eloquently as Arden might sing. "If you will give this to me, half my time I will be a *willing* Imperial Consort, Sovereign. I will appear to the people, attend court."

He thought to catch her another way, dangling bait he thought she might not resist. "What of Jerla? Would you abandon him for days on end?"

"You are not going to get your way in this, Sovereign. Not if you want me to pretend to be happy."

Sovereign had so much more to gain from this than she did. They both knew that. It did not mean he liked it. "I can't trust you, Sigil. We must be honest with each other."

"Do not make me desperate." And there it was, her violence flashing deep in those chilly eyes. "Next time I might kill you."

The look he gave her was not one of sadness or anger. It was a look of pure love. "I'm going to give you what you want."

Sigil released her breath… she felt *free*.

Sovereign had more to say. "But, for now, you will return to the citadel. I would enjoy your company tonight—your willing, complacent company. Save the violence for another."

She was drained of violence thanks to the silent, scarred Lord Commander who'd knocked out her teeth and broken her jaw in their brawl. Sigil found herself staring at him. "Fine."

Sovereign took her chin, and drew her face back toward him. He made her meet his eyes while he drove home something his projected feelings felt was a very important point. "Be cautious with Tiburon, beloved."

Humming disagreement, Sigil offered a rare, dangerous grin. "Why? He and I are the same thing. You must know that. Dr. Saniel made us the same."

The Emperor was not going to elucidate, only warn. "She made him something else."

Chapter 10

A wall of windows framed the bland cityscape carved out of Irdesi's mountain range. Eyes unseeing, Sigil looked up decrepit, beige flotsam, at black banners snapping stark in the streets, distracted by the feel of another's hand toying with her hair.

Warm at her back, the Emperor asked, "Might we talk a little longer?"

That was the third time Sovereign had made such a request since she'd willingly followed him into the palace. Each moment silence came, every instance where he lost her attention, he would ask again and she'd respond with, "We can talk."

He pressed a bit closer. "Who is the Convert—"

Sigil's shoulders stiffened. Now he was just annoying her. "You know Elba's name, her rank, her history. Do not insult me, Sovereign, by pretending otherwise. Tiburon told you where I was."

Strong fingers tangled against her scalp, Sovereign pulling just enough to draw icy eyes to meet his. "What is it about her that drew your attention?"

"The baker's mind is"—she paused, choosing her words carefully—"soothing to be near. Quiet enough that I can ignore all the Convert babble your Adherents polluted her with. She's friendly. She showed me kindness, having no idea who I was—

wanting nothing in return. The only other person who'd treated me that way was Que."

Sovereign's fingers went to the knots binding a pilgrim's rags to Sigil's shoulder. He began to pull at the laces, completely ignoring her mention of the dead Axirlan. "Adherents merely exist to see you protected. You imagine enemies out of accomplices."

Feeling the knot give, the slide of her dirty cloak being pulled aside, Sigil turned her attention once again out the window. "They exist to assure your godlike stature through a pseudo-religion based on lies."

Mouth warm on Sigil's exposed shoulder, Sovereign asked, "And which part is lies?"

Talking was less appealing if he was going to play games.

Sigil's annoyance grew obvious. "If you have a point, Sovereign, make it."

Teeth grazing her nape, an arm circling her middle to warmly palm a breast, Sovereign created an embrace she recognized as a potential restraint, assuming his next words he anticipated would anger her. "If I were to tell you Adherent preaching is not untrue—at least in the basic sense—I am convinced you will not take it well."

Sigil curled her lip and cackled. "I am not the compassionate savior of Converts."

Sovereign's hold tightened. He spoke as if serious. "Your part in their creation is greater than you realize. At the Cathedral, Elba told you—in so many words—that you reside inside them all. Her claim was not an Adherent lie. Conversion serum is a virus created from your fetal cells. It attacks its host and alters key parameters in human DNA, making them susceptible to herd dynamics and suggestion from beings they recognize on a cellular level as their superiors."

His hold tightened fractionally—a strange blend between a hug for comfort and a reminder he was stronger should she think to fight. "Some Adherents would argue they are your offspring—a subspecies edging toward a hive mind that can be further conditioned to mimic our race. Though your virus is milder than those created from males of our kind, our influence—should they survive it—is much more direct and consuming. It serves us all."

If Sovereign had expected an outburst, Sigil was not going to supply one. Asking no questions, making no comments, she stared forward out the window and began chewing her bottom lip.

Sovereign's sigh warmed her ear. "What are you thinking?"

That not once in her existence had her body belonged to her. When she was small, it was a weapon of despots and warmongers—a toy to torment and train. Left to her own devices, it became a vessel for madness. In Sovereign's care, she did not even choose the clothing she was supposed to wear.

Why would they think she'd be surprised they would have done something so sinister with her cells? Fuck, they'd put a machine in her brain.

Sigil could not find it within herself to even feign surprise the Brotherhood had been using her all along. "I am thinking of nothing."

"I had hoped to discuss this after you'd grown comfortable amongst your family. But you have chosen to seek information, and I will not deny you." Sovereign kept the words light, as if his tone might cheer her. "Your friend, Elba, is content. She is content because Conversion saved her from a life of slavery. It gave her purpose, satisfaction to pursue a future she found appealing, while still serving the greater good."

Sigil took a breath, held it until her lungs ached. When she spoke, it all came out on that burning breath. "There are holes in this story, Sovereign. You said fetal cells. How did you have access to such things, yet failed to clone me?"

"Our genetic architecture was constructed in such a way that should we be captured or our corpses recovered, a failsafe assured Alliance enemies would not be armed with Commander Dimitri's magnum opus of military strength. Our bodies degrade almost immediately at death, tissue samples rendered unstable. When our creator, Dr. Saniel, died on Condor, our secrets died with her. But even if it could be done, I would never clone you. Do you understand that, beloved?"

She understood he was circumventing her question. "Answer me. How did you create the virus?"

There was no artifice Sovereign might employ that would hide his discontent. She could sense guilt, shame, intense love, worry, and more as he said, "What we now call the *Serum of Conversion* existed before the Alliance fell. Dr. Saniel created the original infection. It was fed to every member of Project Cataclysm. As all your Brothers have been exposed, you could say that we were the first Converted—the virus switching on a dormant condition so we might recognize our only female should we come into contact. We were predisposed to protect our designed killer should she be sent to thin the ranks."

He had said something to her on Pax: *I cannot help but love you.* Now she understood why. Their obsession, their claims to adore her… none of it was real. Knowing that made her feel something… something she might almost call sad.

Dr. Saniel's safety measure had backfired. It had given a slave army a reason to rebel.

And it had assured a half-mad, tormented little girl would never find peace.

Sovereign caught the look on her face and opened his mouth as if to speak.

She narrowed her eyes, felt anger, and said, "I remember you in the hall on Condor. I didn't like the way you looked at me."

He nodded, looking at her with the exact same expression from all those years ago. "You were conditioned to suffer detachment when you naturally felt a bond. It's the only way they could have inspired you to kill us. But when you looked at me that day, your lip shook. I knew you felt something with one look, something more than the desire to kill."

Lies. Sovereign was telling lies and she didn't have to listen. "That is not what I remember."

"It is fact, Sigil."

"Fact." The word was spat. Twisting out of his hold, she took a step back and gestured to the ridiculous room he kept her in. "What is *fact* in this circus?"

He caught her wrist before she might pace away. Caught it, and pulled her right back into his arms. "You would be surprised at how much fact is layered into our myths."

The best lies always held a hint of truth. Any trained infiltrator knew that. "Then tell me, who are the Soshiia?"

What vibrated from him, what hummed through and around her, was dark emotion hard as steel.

Sovereign did not find her line of questioning appropriate, and if his emotions were any sign, it was not a question he was going to indulge. Yet he answered, and for the first time, his voice held true threat. "They are your only real chance of escaping the Brotherhood. And should you be foolish enough to pursue them, what they would do to you would be beyond any nightmare you survived on Condor."

Sigil's neck craned over her shoulder. She met his eye, unwilling to hide her mean smirk. It felt almost like a challenge, though she was sure he had not meant to intrigue her in such a way.

What was a little more pain?

Free of the Brotherhood?

Hmmmmmm.

Reaching over her shoulder, her fingers tangled in Sovereign's black hair. One yank, a quick twist, and they were eye to eye. "Enlighten me."

"No." It was final. "I won't tempt a child into snatching up poison she believes are sweets."

He could be so infuriating, whilst simultaneously being absolutely no fun!

Releasing her clutch on his hair, she shoved him back, and forced herself to look away from eyes so gripping it almost hurt to see that depth of blue.

Fine, he refused to discuss the Soshiia. There was something else—so glaringly obvious—she could sink her teeth into and burn him with. "It's the serum that made you think you love me."

"No."

Mouth sour, Sigil wondered aloud, one-hundred percent bratty cunt. "I'm unaccustomed to feeling pity."

Sovereign took her nape so quickly she barely felt her hair move. He took it and he pressed his fingers flush to her spine as if daring her to give him a reason to squeeze. "Don't imagine we were unaware of what the draught was before we swallowed it. Decades of intel, of watching, of plotting… we knew practically every last Alliance secret. Swallowing your virus was willingly done by each of us—planned for. *We wanted you!* Days later, I entered the labs and changed you just enough."

It hit her like a ton of bricks. The Brothers were not the only ones poisoned. "With a serum made from you…"

It was to be a two way addiction. That was the reason his physical release had such power over her, why her body craved him and her mind played tricks on her when he was gone. The bastard!

Sovereign tightened his grip and spoke like the domineering Emperor he had made himself. "We were all reborn together, made new."

It wasn't anger, not exactly, that she felt in that moment. What she did feel, she had no name for. She felt like a little girl again. That same scrappy little freak who had long ago tried to guess at the day's torture. "And you just *knew* how to make a serum?"

His grip on her nape continued, Sovereign's thumb running down the length of her neck. "We had a mole in her labs. But there is no point pretending our version wasn't flawed. No living mind in over a century has been able to match the genius of Dr. Saniel." He wasn't sorry, but he was unhappy his strategy had been less than perfect, he projected that clearly enough. "High Adherent Corths did his best."

"You told me he was only a child when the Alliance fell."

"A brilliant mind is a brilliant mind." Seeing her concentrating, knowing each developing conclusion was incorrect, Sovereign added, "You were created to tempt me, Sigil. But we must be honest with ourselves. We cannot prove it was the draught that inspired my adoration for the female secluded from us. I had years to think on it as you grew. That day in the hall, all my previous aspirations for our attachment solidified. Love at first sight is a concept hailed by even the ancients who thrived long before humans destroyed Earth. Why can the same not apply to us?"

Sigil could see through sentiment, because she felt none. "Because Dr. Saniel's draught was designed to inspire that feeling. When Karhl saw me in the yard, when he tried to help me, I felt it from him too—that obsessive *infection*. Arden broadcasted the same impression."

Running through a century of memory in the blink of an eye, one stark divergence stood out. Sigil scowled, puzzling over the difference. "Tiburon, he—"

Resentful at the sound of that name, Sovereign interjected. "Is… immune to *any feeling*, draught or no. Before you were designed, he was altered to belong to someone else, and she didn't want to divide his affection."

What Sovereign hinted at, Sigil found all too easy to believe. Easy and disgusting. "He belonged to Dr. Saniel…"

Shame, disconcertion, Sovereign did not try to hide these things. "Not originally. But by then, he'd been reassigned."

Because Tiburon had been the leader of Project Cataclysm once, usurped by an improved model and made into some type of pet by the very woman Sigil watched him massacre. From esteemed soldier to sex slave, the parallel to her life was too familiar. "And because, unlike you, he isn't compelled to adore me, you question his intentions despite his history of loyalty. *He isn't one of you...*"

"He can't love you. He can only love her... and you killed her." Sovereign's hand slid to Sigil's hip, giving her the opening to shift away should she choose to. "His purpose now is less refined than what the rest of us desire."

The more she heard, the less Sigil wanted to know. Tiburon's history wasn't her business—just as the way he'd tried to help her escape Condor long ago was not for Sovereign to know.

The object of their discussion made himself known. Tiburon cleared his throat and leaned his body against the distant archway.

"I hear you telling tales." Smug, smiling like a shark, he asked, "Think to scare her from me, do you, Brother?"

The disfigured Lord Commander did not hesitate to approach, to wrap a callused hand tight around Sigil's upper arm and pull her from the Emperor's grip.

She was caught between them.

Tiburon sneered, meeting her eyes and making it clear his history gave him no shame.

"Unsalvageable. That's the slander Sovereign is hinting at." Charmed eyes flashed toward his leader, Tiburon smirking. "A harsh title used to label broken Converts. Considering the same applies to our little slut, here, maybe a sweeter word can be found. How about *transfigured*? That sounds pretty, doesn't it? After all, Sovereign's imperfect serum was unsuccessful in doing anything more than damaging Saniel's greatest masterpiece." Those deadly eyes went back to the female measuring his every breath. "You hear that, Sigil? What a mismatched pair we make, and how very threatened they are by it. Whatever we feel for each other… is genuine. I can't tell you the amount of delight this situation has given me over the last century."

Sovereign pulled Sigil closer to his body, projecting his temper like a blaring trumpet. "Leave."

"Let go of your Emperor, Sigil." Tiburon yanked her back, his eyes fixing on his Brother. "I cannot contest a direct order, none of us can—each of us were designed to obey the chain of command. So release your hold on him and come with me. I am eager to have my turn in your company."

There was the sound of hurried steps before Karhl's thick arm wound around Tiburon's throat. Monotone, he said, "Let her go, Tiburon. You've made your point."

Whatever that point might be, Sigil suspected it was not the most apparent one. No other Brother had dared to enter that chamber, though Sigil sensed many edging nearer as if warned two of their elites quarreled over their female.

Feeding off so much animosity, her lip curled, and she peeled Tiburon's fingers from her arm. "Your turn, huh? Tiburon, will you close your eyes while you fuck me? Do you intend to picture Dr. Saniel?"

The male outright laughed, unconcerned Karhl had yet to release his throat.

Sovereign's touch fell all over her: he stroked as if looking for injury. Or was it that he wanted the other man to see his hands roam where they would? Lips were at her ear, the Emperor's words were gently insistent. "It is cruel to mock him, beloved. Tiburon is still your Brother, and a great warrior who sacrificed to reshape the universe for you."

The two were playing some kind of game with each other, and using her as both bait and prize. Moss green eyes narrowed and Tiburon simpered and boldly met her gaze. But his emotions contradicted his appearance. Deep down, he was disgusted.

Looking to the giant at his back, to Lord Commander Karhl, Sigil washed her hands of all of their petty squabbles, preferring to choose neither. "Karhl."

One name, spoken on a sigh, and the tableau was forced to end.

The white-haired warrior set Tiburon free and held out his hand to the woman. "Come, young one. You are hungry and need rest. Let us go see to such things."

The coolness of his temperament poured through her, Sigil reaching out so he might remove her from the chamber. "I am hungry."

Karhl took her hand. "Nor have you slept in days. You shall do so by my side once bathed."

Sovereign did nothing to dissuade Karhl's course, releasing his grip on Sigil's wrist, yet trailing his touch over her fingers as if he did not really wish to let her go. He left her with one promise. "Tomorrow you will return to me."

She left the room on the arm of a male both infamous and revered throughout galaxies for the genocide of billions. In that moment, compared to what was behind her, Sigil was certain Karhl was the lesser of three evils.

Stretching—arms over her head, silken sheets at her back—Sigil arched into the touch of Karhl's roughened palm skimming over her flat belly. He had stroked her for over an hour, watching as his attention hardened the tips of her breasts, pinkened her skin, even before his female had awakened.

The woman bowed again while he kneaded her hip. Whether she meant to or not, it brought her perfect breast near enough he might taste. One languorous lick, that's all he offered her pert nipple, abrading the puckered thing only with the tip of his tongue.

She enjoyed it.

Dipping thick fingers lower, watching Sigil's lips part on a perfect intake of breath, Karhl found her dripping wet.

"You wake aroused?"

He wasn't expecting an answer from the sleepy woman. Not when his finger stole forward, twisting about inside her. She grew even more slippery, cooing soft noises and wiggling her toes.

It was perfect to see her this way, worth every moment of physical frustration he'd felt at the Water Palace.

Pale fingers popped free of her passage so the Lord Commander might taste and consider.

With loss of touch, his Sigil reached for his hand, pulling his fingers from his lips so she might place them back to where her clit peeked from its pierced hood.

The female's impatience inspired the most minuscule of smirks, Karhl freeing his wet fingers to trace lazy circles around rosy nipples instead. "I imagine these swollen with milk." Sea-glass eyes left her tits, waiting to see if the female might speak. "I long to drink from you..."

They were in her bed, the massive tree branching high above them, the ostentatious decoration blocked from view when Karhl leaned down and sucked a ripe breast into his mouth.

Sigil's hand threaded into white ropes of hair. She pulled his head from her breast, stared as her nipple popped from wet lips. It looked as if she might speak, but could not find the words.

Something like regret hung between them, had tormented him since she'd asked him to leave her alone. But there had been no Brother inside her in several days, and he knew she did crave his attention.

He wanted to be the one to pleasure her now. On his terms, with her full acceptance.

Limpid eyes adored, Karhl asking softly, "Would you prefer I call for Sovereign?"

"I gave him my word I'd be a willing Imperial Consort." Was that a flash of anger in her eyes?

Not acceptable.

"Young one, your body responds to me. It has from the first time I touched you." Imprinting his fingers into the curve of her hip, rising above her, Karhl continued, "But I will not make love to you because you bear a sense of obligation. If I were to oblige that incorrect assumption, it would cheapen my faith in your eyes. Only let me in your body because it's what you desire."

He wanted her desperately as more than just a subordinate assisting Sovereign's agenda. Everyone had their part to play in this, and he had played his. He had helped Sovereign fuck her, twice, gained the pleasure of her mouth once, but this moment was not about the Imperial Consort and her condition.

It was about a woman he'd loved for a century. The only female he'd ever felt any inclination toward no matter the thousands he'd fucked. If she came to him in resignation, it would leave a scar inside his body Karhl was certain would never heal.

His erection sat heavy on her thigh, leaking, aching he was so hard. Sigil's attention had been drawn to its studded length.

Sigil started at his cock, she stared and grew merciless. "What if I want you to fuck me? Must I beg you the way Sovereign demands I do?"

Karhl cocked an unimpressed brow. "Is that what he does?"

Frowning, Sigil lost the traces of her excited flush. "No… yes. Maybe."

"I've watched you mate him. The violence…" Karhl ran his lips over hers, desiring her to long for him. He would give her his body as a play thing if she wished, but they could share so much more if she would allow him to give it to her. "That will not be what we share."

To prove his point, Karhl slipped several fingers inside her dripping slit. Sharply hooking her pubic bone, he dug in so he might reach a wondrous buried nerve and strum it.

Like a marionette on strings Sigil gasped, squirmed, danced, making noises that made his cock jerk. Mouth, neck, ear, nipples—he sucked, chewed, and tasted, grinding his palm against her clit, fingers rubbing hard inside her to stroke a place he was sure no other lover had discovered.

When her legs began to twitch, his little Sigil crying out before orgasm might send her past sleepy delirium, Karhl's manic touch grew rough.

That hint of pain and she lost all control. The mattress grew wet beneath her, his hand dripping from her gush of fluids. Soothing the passage that clenched and wept, Karhl further tempted the woman who'd grown pliant, who panted, who he hoped might be seduced into willingness to let him do as he pleased.

There were so many things he could teach her.

He didn't want her to beg, but he wanted her to desire *him* and the thing only he might offer her.

And he knew only one way to show her.

If the Lord Commander was not feasting between her legs, he was devouring her breasts, those same fingers working inside her to manipulate strange nerves. He brushed aside her touch each time Sigil thought to reach for the pierced organ grown purple with the need to fuck. It was not until she was slick with sweat that he stroked his crown through her folds. Up and down her slit, letting those metal piercings catch and tease her labia.

Sigil angled her pelvis in offering, she moaned. But he would not align and enter her.

"Karhl, you told me you didn't want me to beg." Panting, needy, she whined, "Stop teasing and put your dick inside me already."

He laughed.

Sea-glass eyes held hers, Karhl bracing his arms beside her head. "I told you I did not need you to beg, and I meant it. My claim that I would not take you unless you wanted *me* was sincere. Sovereign can serve—"

Her claws dug into his shoulders. "If you try to climb off me to go fetch Sovereign, I will kill you."

This was his moment, his chance to have her. "If you look me in the eye, if you say my name as I breach you, I will show you secret pleasures no one else can give you."

She looked about ready to eat him, yet sighed his name like a lover. "Karhl."

Once it was said, his face turned dark, fiery with the passion of a demon ready to devour another's soul. That bulbous, pierced organ butting her gate was not offered gently. He snapped forward to fill her so sharply she yelped and her back scoured over the sheets.

Had he done such a thing to a human, he would have torn her. His Sigil's cunt on the other hand, swallowed him up because she was made for him.

Had she been lesser, Sigil might have been frightened by the change that came over his features, his mood, and his body.

Instead, she reveled in it as only his true mate could.

He roared as he fucked her, that jabbing pierced cock internally attacking the very flesh his fingers had made sensitive and swollen. And it felt so fucking good that Sigil's eyes rolled back, her fingers gripping his ass to urge deeper penetration.

The second it seemed her pussy might draw tight and orgasm, he made her wait, altering his rhythm to unsettle her senses. He found every sweet spot, his tongue in her mouth and his fingers dancing over her body.

He could give her a fucking unlike any she'd ever known—unique in its calculated physiology. Sigil was made docile, spreading eagerly, and willing to lie beneath him. She showed no temper, didn't bite to harm or scratch to draw blood. Instead, she licked at him and whimpered. She stroked and urged.

And the usually reticent Lord Commander cooed out nasty words as he promised lust and salvation like fresh water to a woman trapped in the desert. He spoke filth to her in languages that had long since died.

He held her on the cusp of explosion, until she was a sobbing mess.

Overloaded, her moans so shrill the city must have heard, Karhl gave a smile that was all teeth. He changed the angle back to punish the spongy flesh on the roof of her cunt, savoring when Sigil arched like one possessed.

One flick of his finger twisting her clit and what had been a powerful orgasm became all-out seizing.

This, watching her weep for him, this was what he'd spent over a century practicing to achieve.

When her throat gave out, her mouth hung open on a silent scream.

He'd killed human females he'd brought to this moment. Their primitive brains short-circuiting and turning to mush. But his Sigil, her eyes were full of life and beautiful madness.

He would make her an addict, give her things the others couldn't.

Her wild gaze was on him just as he'd hoped. She saw him, felt his cock in her, and mouthed his name.

Karhl.

Everything but his love was washed away—just as her pussy was washed when Karhl gushed inside her.

He kept pumping through his release, displacing more of his come with each thrust. Sovereign could fill her later, Karhl's seed did not need to serve that purpose now. Now, what mattered was bringing her down slowly from such great heights.

He rubbed his body against her sweat-slicked skin, groaning like a dying man until her cunt was sloppy with his semen, until her thighs stank of him.

And his sweetness returned while her mind floated somewhere free. Buried hilt-deep, soft kisses were pressed on her lips, soft words of love formed at her ear.

She was so far gone, that to her it may have been poetry he whispered. It may have been an update on Irdesian border expansion. Sigil had yet to wake from her daze.

"...forever."

She managed the barest of breaths. "What?"

Smug, Karhl dipped his tongue past her lips and swept her mouth with his flavor. His weight pressed down on her belly, his pierced cock still resting against her womb. "Giving myself to you was the greatest moment of my life."

She seemed to grow shy from his words. Spent yet bewitched, she asked, "Where did you learn how to do that?"

"I have practiced on many human women in anticipation of our union. Several of the techniques I learned after claiming the Vuul Palace's famous archives. Their manuals on sexual method were… intriguing."

"And the Vuul?"

"There are no Vuul." Because Karhl had seen every last one of them destroyed as soon as infiltration had uncovered the population was highly resistant to Conversion. Not a single child had been left to cry in its cradle.

And never for a moment had he regretted a single life.

Aware her pussy must be sore, that the occasional fluttering around his cock was her nervous system's desperation to find equilibrium, did not lead him to show mercy. Whatever damage he'd done would heal while they were still united.

But suddenly she seemed eager to pull away. "And how many worlds, how many Vuuls, have you eradicated?"

Karhl, still inflamed by adoration, pinned her savagely and growled, "As many as it takes to assure you, your children, and our people, will be safe in a treacherous universe. Believe me when I say that your skittishness on the subject will alter the instant you feel love for something fragile that could be taken from you, young one. What wouldn't you do for your child?"

"I don't have a child."

He looked at her as if he meant to invoke the name Jerla. Instead, Karhl rocked his hips and watched her gasp. "But you will, soon."

Lips petulant and pouty, he kissed with great enthusiasm, and when she calmed, he grew gentle as a lamb. "Though I have yet to discuss my suspicion with Sovereign, I believe conception resulted from our previous group mating. Your chemistry has altered, and you have been exceptionally *difficult* lately."

He'd meant the slander as the highest praise, but she had missed his rare moment of teasing.

Sigil frowned at the mention of a baby. She even failed to disguise the look of fear that crossed her face. "You're wrong."

Comfort he would gladly offer her. Karhl knew in his heart that all would be made right between the Brotherhood and their female once she was with child.

"We shall see." How proud the man could look even while offering practically no expression. "And you will be so happy to hold her."

Sigil allowed the process, Dryden and his Convert attendants dressing her in what was deemed appropriate attire for the Imperial Consort. The white gown was heavy and uncomfortable, enough decorations having been stabbed into her hair that—like the deeply satisfied male watching from the corner—she jingled with each minuscule movement.

Karhl had personally bathed her, prepared himself beside her in a fresh uniform Dryden had carried in.

Sigil had told Sovereign she would be a willing Imperial Consort. Now she was to walk out the massive gateway of the family quarters and parade through gawking subjects.

She was going to be sick.

The sooner it was done, the sooner she could go back to the city—near the baker's quiet mind and hide from all of these men.

The attendants helped her off the dais, Dryden swearing she was a vision.

Arden was not there to agree.

So long as *Quinn* was camouflaged under the paint, Sigil would respect the ridiculousness of it. For once scrubbed clean, her hair set free of the cement worked through it, no court retainer would know her.

It made bearing the weight of a solid metal sunburst on her head far more tolerable.

Picking at the skin around her fingernail, Sigil said, "They must be done by now. I want to get this over with."

Dryden interceded, smiling as if everything wonderful was his doing. "I will be with you, should you need guidance. Ask me anything."

Many nasty retorts sat stinging her tongue, Sigil swallowing them down. "Isn't that Arden's job?"

Dryden bowed gallantly, his robes swishing. "The Herald was required for a sensitive diplomatic mission, Sigil. I am afraid he is not here."

Sigil stopped her parade toward the door, the train of her dress hitching. If Arden was gone, did that mean she would have to deal with Dryden in his place?

The High Adherent grated on her nerves. As did his over-groomed brand of beauty. She made her opinion of him clear with a sneer. "When will he come back?"

The sparkle in Dryden's eyes made his joy at the new dynamic obvious, and his obviousness to her disdain annoying. "Sovereign may be better able to answer that question."

Ignoring the smiling sycophant, Sigil scowled at the Lord Commander. "Karhl, where is Arden?"

"Arden has gone to serve as ambassador before the Tessan Authority. It will be some time before he returns."

If the Empire was in talks with the Tessans, Arden seemed the natural choice for Herald. But he had been useful to her... and Sigil felt strange to hear he would not be around.

The males gave her no time to frown.

The bronze portal spread wide, Karhl setting her fingers on his arm as escort.

There were no humans near the family wing, only the occasional smiling Brother standing guard. Many more she sensed but could not see.

Through galleries and anterooms, chambers and halls, Karhl led her. And then there were humans.

The farther they went, more overdressed Converts accumulated. Watching her every step, Irdesi's highest ranking retainers whispered and stared. They began to follow where she went.

The last room was by far the largest, packed and humming with shushed conversation. In that place Sigil ignored all others, because only one had all her attention—a woman with soft grey hair.

A blue sash hung from the matron's shoulders, and unlike most other high ranked ladies, her jewels were few and far between. Sigil would have never given her notice if not for one key thing. The woman held the little hand of Jerla, whose tail flicked happily in match to his grin.

He was thrilled to see her. "You look funny!"

Sigil studied the child for any sign of trauma, and found only a scrubbed clean little boy dressed in Imperial black. "Do I?"

Jerla repeatedly shifted his weight from one foot to the other, practically bounding like a bug. "My room is HUGE. Outside there is lots of water that falls down and makes the air wet. But there are no trees..."

Robotically quoting what had once been drilled into her brain, Sigil reached out a hand so Jerla might come to her. "Irdesi Prime is a planet of rock and water, chosen for strategic purposes in the system's relation to long ago unconquered human governments. The atmosphere is filtered by algae and moss."

Jerla was still too enthusiastic to recognized the Imperial Consort's silent command to step away from the old woman. "The Emperor says we get to see *the fracturing*. Lady Belloy told me it was even more exciting than the waterfall outside my window."

Lady Belloy? Sovereign had mentioned her before... and her name had shown up more than once in Arden's histories.

Icy eyes darted back toward the human touching her Jerla, and measured the older woman's gracious smile. "I have heard of Belloy's spouse. You are Matron Delphine, the Convert wife granted children with Sovereign's Brother."

"Twins, yes."

Looking over every last inch of the matron, Sigil wondered why that human was more important than the rest. Why she was allowed near? Why she was the exception? Why could she wear blue when all others in the room wore black? "You have cared for Jerla since he woke?"

"It was my honor, Imperial Consort."

The boy seemed happy, his tail swishing in a sure sign of contentment. "She can't fly, but we played games with numbers. I know twenty now."

Face blank, Sigil blinked, and further extended her palm to the child. "Well done, Jerla. Thank Lady Belloy and take my hand."

Matron Delphine interjected. "At a later time, may we discuss his course, Imperial Consort? Tutors must be chosen to suit the path you intend him to walk."

Jerla's little hand gripped the painted fingers Sigil outstretched. He squished up his nose upon touching her skin. "Why are you covered in white dust. Why is everyone quiet? I want to go outside."

His chatter made her nervous.

Yellow eyes stared up, Jerla's brow dipping. "What's wrong?"

There were so many humans in the halls, all of them watching her. All of them were a threat.

Snatching Jerla up so he might rest on her hip, Sigil found her heart racing. It calmed a bit when a yellow-scaled tail wrapped around her middle.

His little hands smeared the script her attendants had painstakingly painted between her breasts. Her white paint made a mess of his black clothes.

Lips at the indentation of his ear, Sigil whispered, "Be cautious, Jerla. Not everyone who smiles is a friend."

Reaching up his scaled mouth to coolly brush her ear, Jerla mimicked action by whispering, "She's nice."

Sigil's eyes bored into the placid expression of the matriarch. No drop of suspicion was concealed from look or tone as she accused, "You've already won him over."

A steady reply was offered in return. "The boy was well chosen, Imperial Consort. He loves you."

There was that word again. Those four letters that made men mad.

Sigil turned the weight of her skull to see the child leaning into her shoulder. The little one's forehead pressed in, his snake-like face hidden as he squeezed a great big hello.

"I love him too." Pitiless eyes darted up and circled the crowd, Sigil's face one of severe warning while she employed *that* word. "I love him greatly, and I will crush any who think to make use of that love. I would harm your children, your house, your people. I would destroy anything a Convert heart might hold dear, until you were nothing but dust forgotten in history."

No one in the assembly dared meet her eye, all genuflecting just enough to cover shock at the Consort's outburst. But hearts were nasty things, and the room was pinging with several minds that Sigil knew not to trust.

No living thing was passive when more could be gained. Everyone wanted an edge.

The city below might be saturated in ideal, but Irdesi's court was Pax, only much prettier with their rules and costumes.

Now, Sigil was no longer the invisible pleasure slave. She was Drinta.

"Imperial Consort," Karhl retook her arm, allowing little Jerla space between them. "If we linger, we shall miss what Sovereign would share with you."

He had not called her 'young one,' and the formal alteration hung between them.

Everyone had a part to play.

Drawn forward, the final set of grand doors opened onto the grandest terrace on the planet. Outside, Sovereign waited. As did the population of Irdesi Prime crowded down below.

A little boy who adored without question tugged her clothes. "Look at all those people!"

The Emperor called her forward. "Come now, beloved. Step to the balustrade so everyone can see you."

Sigil obeyed, her susurrating steps confined by ridiculous clothes.

The air was blazing with cheers, the noise so loud Jerla's excited chatter could not be heard. Looking to the boy in her arms, seeing his state of bliss, she smiled.

The sky broke, scattering light veining in and out of atmospheric storms. The Converts' hum vibrated through them all until the world felt perfect—until it was even easy to feel the love she'd claimed she bore for the child.

Upturned, inky Tessan eyes looked into hers with so much joy.

That expression sat on his face in the instant of his death. The hum had yet to cease, but pain tore through Sigil's right lung. The boy in her arms sagged forward, a gaping hole in his back.

"Jerla...?" Blood came from Sigil's mouth.

His mind was gone from her reach, the broken thing cradled at her shoulder shot straight through. Though the child had taken the brunt of an assassin's fire, the attack had been well aimed. Wheezing through a collapsing lung, through the fire of torn skin, Sigil stumbled backwards and fell.

The sky was still beautiful.

Chapter 11

Adherents were buzzing frantically in the antechamber of the family wing, arguing amongst themselves and fretting. "She walked back to her rooms with the Tessan child's body in her arms. She walked the entire way bearing a wound that would have claimed the life of any human. The court saw! Those who sought to help her, she harmed."

Another voice broke through the din. "She refuses to give up the body. She won't let Corths attend her."

High Adherent Corths spoke up, focused on his projections, face drawn by concentration. "Sigil knew how to drain a collapsed lung herself. My help was unnecessary and unwanted. If you try to take the boy from her, she will rampage. Allow her to mourn."

"The corpse will begin to rot..."

Tiburon approached with his faction. Indisputably furious, he put an end to the foolishness of chattering priests. "Get out! Go into the city and do your fucking jobs before Sovereign slaughters the entire population singlehandedly!"

His orders were followed at once, yet his scarred face turned its wrath next on Corths. "Ballistic reports offer little information. Shards of the missile broke apart on impact. I need them."

Corths projected a hologram of a body scan. "They're still inside her and the boy. I suspect the pain is keeping her brain functions level. The readouts from her implant... she is calming slowly." As if impressed with the Consort, the male added, "It's a brilliant approach, really."

Tiburon rolled his eyes, let out a beleaguered breath, and marched toward the sealed door. "I'll take them out of her myself."

His hand went to the access panel, the mechanics unnaturally twitching each time he tried to force them. "Open the door, brat!"

One of the lesser Adherents, a low ranking Brother explained. "Her psionics have been holding that door for twenty-seven hours."

"She has been alone in there all this time?"

Corths shook his head. "The Emperor swore to her he would lay the one responsible at her feet. Neither he nor Karhl have returned. But she is not alone. Dryden followed her in."

Tiburon laughed, the sound hollow and cruel. "Then she's killed him." Measuring the younger Brother, the one who held great power in his title yet preferred his lab and experiments, the Lord Commander sneered. "Looks like you've been promoted."

Muted by her implant, wounded and tired, the Imperial Consort could not continue her mental grip against the onslaught when Tiburon took matters into his hands. One violent burst of psionics and he broke her thready hold.

Shoving busted mechanics out of his way, he stormed in.

It was dark, but he could see that the floor was spattered with blood and vomit leading in a trail to the great bed. There she lay, Jerla's stiff body in her arms. The boy's eyes were open, sunken, and the smell of his open chest cavity, repulsive.

Contempt rolled off Tiburon's sharp tongue. "Get up."

"When a Tessan pilgrimages, it's known as going to the sands. The same term applies to their death." Sigil turned her head, matted hair crusted to the pillow. "Jerla was afraid of the sands."

Tiburon scowled. "What have you done with Dryden?"

A filthy finger pointed to the far corner. The shadow of a body lay crushed into the dark.

"That was unwise, Sigil."

Voice flat, Sigil sighed. "He might be alive..."

No way was that lump alive. Just to make sure, Tiburon toed it with his boot. Dryden was indeed, very dead—already decayed into mush. "He was your Brother, Sigil. You've murdered one of our family."

Sigil ran her fingers over the skull of her boy. "Dryden was the unwise one, forcing his way in. He would not leave me alone."

Arms over his chest, Tiburon approached the bed. "That body needs to be incinerated."

Sigil did not agree. "Not yet."

"When?"

"What do you want, Tiburon?"

Focusing on the tatters of bloodstained cloth and torn skin, the Lord Commander was blunt. "What you were struck with was not only cloaked, but unusual. I require the debris in your chest for further diagnostics."

"I know what it was, a *Keppling Heart-Seeker*—a black market modification of Tessan design. Very expensive, difficult to obtain."

"How can you be sure?"

Disdain clouded narrowed eyes. "I lived on Pax."

Sitting at the edge of the mattress, Jerla between them, Tiburon tore back the remnants of Sigil's bodice, feeling around the most obvious of wounds. She let him. Some pieces he pinched with his fingers, two were wrenched out with psionics.

She was bleeding, face white under the paint and gore. After a shaky breath, she said, "There are three more buried deeper. It would be easier to remove them from my back. Just yank them through."

Tiburon had no qualms following her suggestion. But there would be consequences if all things were not considered. "If you don't eat you won't heal."

"I'll eat Dryden."

She was not joking. Still, Tiburon chuckled. "He's no longer fresh, brat."

Before she could respond, he flared his psionics. The remaining fragments erupted from her back, shredding open three new injuries, and leaving her struggling for breath.

When it was done, stern Tiburon disappeared, his smartass condescension having come out to play. "If you're waiting for Sovereign to return with the ones responsible for the death of that child, your wait will be indefinite. If we knew how to differentiate the Soshiia from Converts, they would have been slaughtered already. All *you* had to do to find an agent was stand within fifty paces of one. If you want justice, get off your ass and use your crazy empathic brain to find them yourself. Otherwise, Sovereign will continue to cleanse this entire city. He'll kill them all, your Elba included."

Sigil was in far too much pain to speak, her lung malfunctioning from the latest damage. But her eyes went wide at his words, and she sank her nails into Tiburon's arm.

"That's right, brat. Fight back."

She wheezed. "He wouldn't…"

"It's already begun. Now, get up."

"There is nothing else I can do for this child."

Corths sighed, his patience with humans having never developed to the steady acuity of the deceased High Adherent Dryden. "The Imperial Consort wants you to stay with Jerla."

Lady Belloy looked down at the table, at the small Tessan she'd washed so the corpse might not lay so sadly. "I have done what I can for the boy, but the planet is being cleansed. I should be in prayer, preparing for the passage of my soul from this body."

Pulling fine black fabric over the boy to hide exposed rib bones and a hollowed chest cavity, Corths said, "You might survive the draught."

Lady Belloy gave a tired smile. "I'm an old woman, High Adherent. It is merciful for wives to be given an opportunity to transcend by swallowing the serum of the elite warrior class. But I will not survive it."

It would kill them all, Corths was certain. "You lack faith."

"No." Lady Belloy tucked the blanket around the body, just as she had tucked her children to bed when they had been small. "I have every faith that the Soshiia infection must be stopped. At any cost."

"Agreed." But Corths was not content. A full scale cleansing of a Convert world had not been required in sixty years. The fact one was taking place on the capital planet was a blow. Perhaps that's why he spoke to a human of things better left to the Brotherhood. "Our lady would see the cleansing stopped. It seems her mercy extends beyond what she imagined."

"I agree with our Emperor..."

Now Lady Belloy intrigued Corths, the man arching his brow. "You would die, see millions dead, to assure the removal of what might be only one Soshiia agent?"

"The Imperial Consort was struck before the entire population, almost killed the first night she gave herself to us. And what of my children, my future grandchildren, on other worlds? Should I allow this villain to make an escape, to flee and spread his disease through our great empire?"

"And the children dying in the city right now?"

The old woman nodded, her face one of anguished acceptance. "It is unspeakable what must be done in the name of peace. All Converts know that."

No one stood in her way because no one walked the streets. Soldiers had sectioned off the city by region, stood at posts highly armed. Sigil did not allow them to see her. Irdesi Prime, by all appearances, suffered under occupation. But it was by their own kind—humans were the soldiers aiming weapons at civilians, at people who might be their sister, their son.

Segments that had already felt the hand of the Emperor were just... gone; only craters of burning rubble left in their wake. The smell of smoke burned in Sigil's weak lungs, drove her closer to what could only be the frontline.

The white head of Karhl she saw first. He stood taller than the elite surrounding him, than the Brothers taking orders to lead their own squadrons.

She was not a pretty sight. Not when blood caked the crushed design of her hair, not when the white makeup was smeared into a blur of grey foulness. But Sigil wore the uniform, one Tiburon had helped pulled on her limbs. For that reason alone the soldiers did not shoot her on sight when the female revealed herself.

The night was stygian, smoldering remains doing nothing to increase visibility, but Sigil's voice carried over the tramp of marching boots, over shouted commands. "Stop this, Karhl."

Turning so fast his hair flared, a provoked Lord Commander glowered to see her where she should not be. "Young one."

She cried over the crowd again. "I do not condone this!"

Pushing through the men that separated them, the Lord Commander charged forward. Limpid eyes took in the uniform, the dried bloodstain running from her mouth down her neck. "You should not be here. It is obvious you are still wounded."

She was, but she was also strong enough to start a fight if she had to. "Where is Sovereign? I need to speak with him."

The Lord Commander put a heavy hand on her shoulder, careful to keep the touch light. "I suggest that you do not."

The last thing Sigil desired was to be coddled. Throwing his hand off, she threatened him with every ounce of intimidation she could produce. "You cannot annihilate an entire population in hopes you might ferret out one *Unsalvageable*. What justice is there for Jerla in genocide?"

The man who possessed the patience of the sea, actually growled. "None of this is for Jerla."

Her throat grew tight, icy eyes grew wet. "I know.... I know he was only a tool in the eyes of your family—"

"It is *our* family, Sigil."

Speaking over the interruption, she refused to be silenced. "—but Jerla was mine. I will be the one to hunt those responsible. I will destroy all they love. Do not take that from me!"

"So what would you have us do? Offer rebel agents who successfully and publicly shot our Imperial Consort time to regroup? I can see the entire planet cleansed in less than five days. There will be no escape for them, not with warships orbiting, ready to shoot down any vessel."

"Would you not rather gather intelligence through interrogation?"

"Torture is ineffective against Soshiia."

Every mind could be broken. After all, look at what had become of her. "If you are responsible for the death of one more Convert in this action, Dryden won't be the last Brother I murder today."

The Lord Commander's face went blank.

Karhl stared down at the female; he calculated, he waited. When her fingers twitched and began to spark, the Lord Commander turned, calling over his shoulder. "Come with me."

He led her farther up the field to where fresh fires burned and bodies were stacked for incineration. Women and children, young and old, it made no difference. All their minds were silent.

Wasted life, not one her enemy—not one of them anything to her. "Why do you kill the children? How can they be considered responsible for an assassination attempt?"

Karhl had stopped by her side when Sigil hesitated near another pile of corpses. "Children become adults."

The thought turned her stomach. "And the empire is concerned they will grow up drunk on the desire for revenge."

"It is better to remove the potential problem than feed a latent uprising." Karhl's logic was cold and pragmatic, the way he eyed the dead as unfeeling as the Axirlan he resembled.

"You're wrong—"

A voice came from behind her. "Our history proves he isn't."

It was a voice that sounded nothing like the Emperor who had hunted her, who had taken her from Pax.

Sigil had sensed him, the rage and the violence so harsh it had a physical effect on her. But when she turned to face him, what stood against the smoke wasn't Sovereign. It was a breathing demon.

Walking over a pile of broken bodies, blood dripping from his fingers, Sovereign's eyes burned. "This is not for you to see."

No. The fixed agony, the faces locked in dead screams called out to her—they judged her.

Sigil had committed atrocities, murdered on a whim, wallowing in her madness when it descended. She had played with the bodies of the dead, eaten them, tossed limbs about and reveled in it. She had done those things because she was a monster. "You're no different than me..."

Stepping down, heedless of mashing skulls or crunching bone, Sovereign closed the gap between them, and said, "I am much worse."

He went to embrace her, affection from something so horrid, so bloodthirsty, unexpected.

Sigil startled, froze, breath hitching when he pulled her against him and nuzzled her hair.

It was the feeling coming from inside him, the perversion of it choking her. She was frightened of Sovereign. The fact that she was scared, that she recognized her feelings as such, petrified her further.

When his mouth worked a path near her lips, Sigil whimpered. "Stop."

"Stop?" Sovereign's grip tightened, his voice razor blades. "It is always stop, isn't it? I give you gentleness, you fight. I build you an empire, you hate me for it! I could take you here, on these very dead right now. I could make you, and you couldn't stop me—just like you couldn't stop me on Pax. I could push into your body anytime I wanted." He bit at her mouth, lapped her lips before he shoved the startled woman away. "There is no STOP! There is only wait. Wait while you fuck my Brother. Wait while you mourn a being who never loved you. And I will wait, Sigil. You would be surprised how far my patience will extend. But there is never, ever going to be a *stop*. I don't even think the grave could keep me from you."

She'd tracked his movements, hearing each layer of the monster's shouted threat, and found it was only the two of them left in the circle of the dead's judgment. Karhl had gone, all soldiers having followed.

Smoothing back the tangled black that hung over his eyes, Sovereign straightened to his full height. Even furious, she still found him beautiful, flawless... no matter the corruption of blood or filth.

For some reason, that frightened Sigil more.

She felt small, defenseless in the face of so much power.

And he could see it.

Like crashing waves, his eyes narrowed dangerously. Sovereign took a step toward her.

She backed a step away. "You promised to bring me the ones who hurt Jerla. They are mine to kill. The massacre of millions is not what I want."

Sovereign looked incensed by the way she shrunk from him. "First there was the Soshiia agent on the ramparts upon your arrival to Irdesi. Then, a coordinated attack against our only female—an attack that must have involved many, considering all the possible unknowns a sniper had to counter and prepare for. You could have died! The infection permeates this entire planet and it ends now!"

A little jerk of the head—left to right—a slight negation, was all she could offer when Sovereign's emotions seared and sent her brain to pounding. All she wanted was to put her hands to her ears, as if the internal screams, the roaring crash of too much fury, might be shut out.

Seeing her brow crease, seeing her eye twitch, Sovereign demanded, "The implant, Sigil, is it malfunctioning?"

The space behind her eyes boiled. A drop of blood fell from her nostril. "You're hurting me."

Something in the man changed. He pulled on majesty like a cloak, and in the blink of an eye, his mannerisms altered. Before her stood an Emperor, the fabrication she'd come to know—the thing he'd pretended to be so the demon might appeal and draw her in.

The real Sovereign was far more terrible, beyond her description, and Sigil was lost by the magnitude of him. Stunned, she muttered, "How could Commander Dimitri believe I would have ever been able to kill you? I would not have been able to get within ten paces."

"You kill me every time you turn away, every time I have to force myself not to make a grab for you." His lip curled in an expression very similar to the one Tiburon favored. "You kill me when you look at me as you are now."

"Sovereign." Sigil swallowed, the burn in her throat growing from the smoke. "Please."

He reached out as if to touch her.

Closing her eyes, bracing, Sigil fought every instinct that told her to run.

The bloody hand paused mid-air, fingers curling as the arm was dropped.

His voice was toneless. "Ask yourself why you are afraid right now."

She didn't know what to say, whispering, "I killed Dryden," because she could not admit that he terrified her.

Sighing, Sovereign conceded, "I know you did. I was monitoring you through his communications implant. I am always watching you, always with you even when you share the company of the others."

"If you are trying to ease my anxiety, you're failing."

At that he touched her cheek, palmed it to wipe the blood dripping from her nose away from her mouth. "Perhaps my approach has been too indirect. I've let you formulate and misconstrue. You do not respond well to cautious handling and subtle manipulation. Should I force you? That is what you were conditioned to appreciate."

Sigil was not sure what they were talking about anymore. She wasn't sure of anything in the presence of such a creature. "Order a cessation of the cleansing, Sovereign. I can find the Soshiia. I will help you."

"No."

"Jerla was taken from me." And she would not let the ones responsible be killed in a mass murder—not until she got her taste of them and made them suffer. "Don't take the city from me too."

"They are only humans, beloved. Irdesi Prime could be repopulated and at optimal output within a year."

It wasn't that simple. Had he not told her so a million times? Sigil gritted her teeth. "I'll give you anything you want."

"I want a child," Sovereign was quick to answer, to let his eyes burn.

Sigil glanced away, defeat hunching her shoulders. "I don't know how to give you one."

The smile that bloomed on his face was one of extreme anticipation. "Lay down."

The demon that had crept over her in the ash and gore, the one who'd torn open her uniform and lapped at the blood crusted on her healing chest, was not the man who'd fucked Sigil over and over again since the moment he'd found her on Pax.

He did not let her scratch or bite, he didn't try to console. He took.

Though not with pain. Even when Sovereign spread her thighs he didn't maul. It was a smooth entry, and an almost lazy motion drenching each thrust. If a dragon could stretch in the sun and roll with the utmost pleasure over his horde of coins, Sovereign was that creature.

That is not to say he let her off with any amnesty. His vocal mandates, the way they licked at her ear, were almost too much to bear. "Admit I am stronger."

She was so cold, even lying under a mountain of heat. Shivering, she nodded, as if that might be enough to meet his demand.

"Tell me..."

Those eyes—in the dark they seemed bottomless, a great abyss ready to suck her into nothingness. "You are stronger."

Sovereign thrust deep enough her breath stuttered, her lips parted, and her hips angled for more. He looked to where he joined their bodies, gave her a reprieve from the intensity of his gaze. Fucking her deliberately, watching his cock vanish over and over into his trembling female, he felt her writhe and shudder from his hands and mouth. But she was not doing as he commanded.

Hand knotting into her hair, Sovereign pulled her head back, exposing her neck. Her yelp was ignored, the tensing of her body disregarded. He lapped at her pulse points, at the soft place under her chin. Every weak spot was thoroughly attended to, Sigil stuck staring straight into the flat eyes of a corpse lying right behind her.

"Tell me you recognize what I am, that you're mine in every way."

His hips, that same ruthless easiness, the way his cock stretched and pulled at her, made pleasure weave itself through every nerve... Sigil wanted him to stop making her feel things. His very presence was consuming, his smell—the way she had found herself more comfortable near him than when he was away. But that Sovereign wasn't this Sovereign. That gentle Sovereign had never really existed. That Sovereign's habitual physical seduction, the mindless pleasure he wielded to keep her full of his sperm, had been a ploy.

This Sovereign, this creature who bombarded with desire had no intention of heeding her should she say no. Had she not lain in the dirt when he'd told her to, he would have forced her down and bitten her into a frenzy of need.

Her view changed, Sigil unsure when he'd released her hair or exactly how long she'd stared into his eyes. The feeling of his ass clenching under her palm, of the way his ribs expanded with each breath—she was touching him, learning his muscles, seeking the warmth of his flesh to drive off the chill.

And how he reveled in such attention. "That's right, beloved. Smile at me." The demon grinned, parted his lips to pant. "You don't need the city to sing to remember what you are. That feeling that overwhelms you during each night's Fracturing, that is your love—and it belongs to me."

It was only a response to stimulus, that fluttering in her chest—a response to hunger, followed by fear, followed by the friction of his cock. The sensation was fleeting, coming and going, building and ebbing in time with Sovereign's determined thrusts.

He filled her to the brim and ground his pelvis against her mound. "Tell me that you'll love me."

Spread beneath him, cunt stuffed full, Sigil breathed almost too softly to be heard, "I'll love you."

His tongue was in her mouth, his body full upon her. It took him less than three full thrusts until Sovereign came, crying out her name in perfect pleasure.

The blasting heat that always accompanied his eruption satisfied, but it did not bring her to completion. Lying spread under him, needing friction to relieve her need, she squirmed.

Sovereign did not leave her unattended for long. His eyes commanded her to hold his gaze as he reached between them to run his thumb where she throbbed. He controlled her pleasure, could give it or deny it. He controlled her body in that pile of dirt and ashes.

He always had.

Arching up against the cock plugged deep inside her, starved for more of his touch, she wanted him to burn her away. "Bite me..."

"No."

Unsure why his refusal was all it took for orgasm to crash upon her, Sigil keened, her cunt milking him, drawing his spilled seed deeper.

"It is your custom to retreat into apathy each time you make progress. Such behavior is cowardly and done out of fear," Sovereign growled, the demon blazing in triumph as he pulled out and looked down on the woman he'd fucked amongst the dead. "This time it will not be allowed. Not even as you mourn Jerla."

She remained sedate as he fixed her clothing, covering the breasts he'd licked clean. When he had her dressed, he pulled her to stand and righted his own mussed uniform.

"Will you spare the city?"

Sovereign put a hand over her womb and hummed. His thumb traced back and forth. "I will give you fifteen cycles to find the Soshiia. If you fail to do so, all humans on this world will die."

Chapter 12

Chin in her hand, Sigil cut Sovereign a wary glare. It was not a look of anger, or even suspicion, it was simply another measure of the man at her side.

She did not know this new male, even if she might still taste him in her mouth.

And for some reason, she couldn't tear her eyes away from his form.

He looked like Sovereign, sat with all the assumed arrogance of an Emperor, but for all those past months, the captor who'd sat beside her had been an illusion. Under all that beauty and tender demeanor lay the kind of monster she understood.

He was a stranger, yet so familiar she could tap out the cadence of his heartbeats.

And, there he lounged, cutting a piece of fruit.

Smiling at her attention, Sovereign offered her the first wedge of mangosteen. "Beloved."

He could pretend so casually, wear the mask with such precision. Sigil felt a spark of envy. Being *him* took no effort on his part. Functioning had always been hard for her. It was still hard, even cocooned in that damn palace and kept close to something powerful enough to destroy her with little more than a flick of the wrist.

She opened her mouth, and let Sovereign lay the fruit on her tongue.

The taste and texture were familiar. "I remember this from the Water Palace. It grew on the walls in Spring."

The Emperor nodded, his knife skipping through another bright-white segment.

"It was the first thing you fed me after I woke up." Sigil sat back in her chair, lazy. "Are you trying to draw some sly comparison?"

Sovereign popped a wedge of fruit into his mouth, grinning like a naughty child. "I like mangosteens."

His nonchalance seemed inappropriate considering he'd just fucked her on a pile of corpses.

He'd bared himself in all his horrid power, overcame and conquered so thoroughly Sigil had actually allowed him to carry her back to his palace cradled to his chest like a child. She'd even slept part of the way.

Death and ash no longer greyed their skin because he'd washed it from her.

It was his touch that had braided her wet hair, his hands that pulled a velvet robe over her nakedness, and his fingers he'd entwined with hers as he'd led her to the others.

Karhl and Tiburon sat at the polished onyx table, neither pleased with the show. One was covetous, one was mistrustful. Both were stoic.

Since she'd joined them, Karhl had not once tried to touch her, a thing very unlike him. He, of all the males, seemed most discontented with her enlightenment.

Tiburon openly sneered, drumming his fingers on the table, thoroughly bored and deeply aggravated.

Sovereign was stone. Inside she observed him focusing all that vast mental brilliance into a fine point she found difficult to read. Every other emotion she'd known in him, it seemed he'd fed her, carefully conditioning what she could and could not sense.

The Emperor had armor against her only advantage. Sigil found herself uncertain of what had been real and what had been fabricated.

Tired of being ignored, the white-haired Lord Commander spoke. "How is it you intend to find the Soshiia, young one?"

Sigil blinked, looked from the smirking Emperor as if she'd forgotten others waited in the room. "I am going to sell bread."

Tiburon cocked a brow, thoroughly unimpressed. "And?"

"I will sell this bread while the Imperial Consort makes an appearance. I think we can all expect at least one agent will be in the crowd. When I find him, I'll track him. He will lead me to the others."

The instant grin and low chuckle... Tiburon lost his boredom. "Sometimes you impress me and I forget how horribly misguided you really are. And just who, brat, do you think Sovereign would allow to take your place on that balcony? Though I would enjoy it immensely, fraud of that level would be a scandal once recognized. It would upset the balance of power between factions. And you forget, Converts are fragile. There is no single human on this planet who could support the weight of those clothes, let alone take your place without thinking themselves more important than they are."

Waving off such dramatics, Sigil disagreed. "Does the Brotherhood not have wives? At least one must look like me? Who would even know once she's painted white?"

"Not a single one of them could be trusted," Karhl interjected, hands steepled, frown in place. "Secrets can be kept, Sigil, but some things are unwise. Nothing goes unnoticed at court. Ever."

The argument was pointless. Swiping up a glass of water, she swallowed, took three breaths, and said, "It's a pity Arden isn't here. The Herald would dress up in my clothes himself and parade around if I asked him to."

"Well." Tiburon leaned forward, openly vexed to hear that name on Sigil's lips. "If I were you, I'd be grateful that conniving bastard was sent away."

A furious bark roared from Sovereign. "Tiburon!"

The Lord Commander threw his attention toward the infuriated Emperor. "Oh yes, we all know that *cancer* is your favorite pet. It's the only reason—"

The walls shook. "SILENCE!" Sovereign seethed. Hands to the table, his mass leaned forward as if his jaw might unhinge and swallow Tiburon whole. "What is it that you think to accomplish in this?"

They were wasting her allotted time. "I know of a human who will serve in my place on that balcony—one unknown to the court; one who does not crave power."

Tiburon knew of whom she spoke, enlightenment breaking upon his face. "Your baker, Elba."

"She will do as she's told, and she will do it because she loves your empire."

Sovereign drew out the deeper meaning of Sigil's claim so the woman would have to address it. "And she loves you. Does that not also make this your empire?"

Pulling her hair over her breast, Sigil strangled the braid, and grew sad. "Pax was mine. Que was mine."

"And we are all yours." Dark brows dipped, Sovereign's smile vanished. He took the last bite of fruit. "Time and practice will change your sentiment."

Sigil eyeballed his empty hands, her belly unsatisfied even after so much food. "I am still hungry."

The final dish at the table was pushed before her, Sovereign's eye glittering with something unsettling. He cocked a brow at her. "Elba will serve in your turn. And you"—he cupped his hand to her cheek, pulling her lower lip down so he might trace the edges of her teeth with his thumb. He pressed his finger down until a drop of his blood welled to drip in her mouth. At one hint of the taste, Sigil closed her eyes and sucked. He groaned, eased closer, and purred—"You will sell her bread."

The taste of him was delicious. He let her gnaw, watching her, and counting her every last lick.

Sovereign projected encouraging admiration, yet pulled his bloody finger away. "You are tired, beloved."

A red drip thought to escape the corner of her mouth, Sigil's pink tongue darting out to catch it.

There was nothing innocent in the way Sovereign gloated to find her openly aroused. She licked her lips and leaned closer as if ready to take another bite out of him. Yet, she hesitated, her next exhale shaken.

Breath growing unsteady, throat tight, Sigil found her hands shook.

She no longer looked at Sovereign, but at the table, the food, the place settings. From the corner of her eye she could see it, the very knife Sovereign had used to slice fruit.

Light played off the polished blade, winking at her.

It spoke to her of more blood.

She had not even felt the pulse of psionics that dragged it to rest in her fist, had not recognized that she stared at it for several seconds before her arm shot out in a great sweep.

She went for Sovereign's throat.

A cry of pain passed her lips and Sigil found that same shaking hand lay imprisoned against the obsidian table.

Her wrist had been broken with the speed and force of Sovereign's response.

Fist in her hair, his lips at her ear, he growled a firm, "No."

Sigil didn't know why she'd done it.

She didn't know anything but the roiling nausea growing in her belly.

The pressure on her scalp ceased, Sovereign's fingers inching downward to trace the bones in her neck. Something beyond her was still fighting for the knife, the muscles of her arm twitching with the effort.

He found the spot and pinched.

It was immensely comforting.

Her eyes went half-lidded, her arm ceasing its jerking in Sovereign's immovable restraint.

"Now, let go of the knife, Sigil."

She did, opening her palm.

The blade was instantly confiscated by Karhl.

Lowering her lashes, Sigil closed her eyes. She made herself breathe deeply just as Que had taught her. But, the sound of blood in her ears, the way she swallowed… she was not fully in control.

Tiburon, equally impressed and astounded, spoke of her as if she was not there. "She moves so fucking fast."

Sovereign agreed. "Yes, she does. Note her involuntary response—there are subtle cues." The Emperor kneaded the flesh of her neck, drawing her near him as he explained. "Minute muscle spasms, fixation, an expression of regret. Isn't that right, my love?"

Even under his touch, Sigil's cold sweat and intense discomfort would not abate. "I'm going to be sick…"

"Shhhhhh. Come here." Dragged from her chair to the cradle of his lap, Sovereign brought her injured wrist to his lips. "I am not angry."

Sigil was not listening, not with her cheek to his collarbone and his hands in her hair. All she heard was his heartbeat mingling nicely with the pulse of her pained wrist. It swept her up, carried her away.

Snorting, Tiburon chuckled. "The brat's fallen asleep."

Tracing his touch over his beloved's face, Sovereign looked down at the exhausted female napping in his arms. "Tomorrow will not be a good day."

Karhl had watched, he too had calculated. "Which is why I intend to stay with her tonight. Statistics prove she retains stronger mental balance after sleeping in my care."

Tiburon shifted to glare at the formidable white-haired soldier at his side. "And leave all the work in my lap again so you can play house and fondle the hellion? No. Our duties are triple now that she convinced Sovereign to stop the cleansing. The Soshiia will see this as a sign of weakness. They will muster for a second push, even as she picks their agents off."

"Tiburon is correct." Lifting his gaze, Sovereign addressed the waiting brothers. "Sigil only bargained for the human lives within the capital's borders. That is all. The cleansing of Irdesi Prime will continue. Every rock outside the city I expect purified before I see either of you in the flesh again."

Tiburon apparently loved the idea, grinning as he said, "You'll piss her off when she uncovers your cheap trick, Sovereign."

The Emperor did not agree. "I'm increasing the odds of our success. All potential Soshiia agents must be eradicated, the leadership driven into the capitol. I will keep Sigil safe and distracted. You"— Sovereign growled as if failure would result in their slow death—"will find the pair of them and deal with the problem. They must be captured and removed before Sigil might be compromised."

"Agreed." Tiburon raised his glass.

Karhl was of like mind. "Agreed."

"What of the child?" Tiburon looked pointedly at Sigil's stomach. "Are you going to tell Sigil she's pregnant before she might... I don't know... expose herself to radiation or poison her body with lead?"

Putting his large palm over her belly, Sovereign softly smiled. "The subject will be fully broached tomorrow."

"It better be..."

Chapter 13

Flour, a light dusting, coated everything. Sigil traced a finger through it, writing the name *Jerla* over and over on the windowpane. "We must leave soon for the square."

The weather was almost uncomfortably cold, small bits of ash still raining down outside. When it grew time for the fracturing, those who'd survived Sovereign's initial purge would be eager to gather in the open air. Human Converts would want to huddle, wrapped up in their silly faith to cheer the woman who'd found them worthy of saving from the cleansing.

Sovereign leaned against the wall, his pilgrims' rags concealing his beauty and rank. But his charm and persuasive abilities, were openly applied upon their hostess—as if Elba were the queen and he the peasant. "Your bread is delicious. I can see why the Imperial Consort favors it so highly."

Under her customary layer of flour, Elba's freckled cheeks blushed scarlet. "I'm honored, Emperor."

As if they could be casual with one another, Sovereign held out a crust of bread to his pensive female. "Beloved, would you like to try it?"

Sigil's icy eyes did not abandon her childish drawings on the glass. "No."

"Are you still feeling unwell?"

"Yes."

Elba was not offended. Reaching for a pitcher, she filled an earthen mug. "Would you like something to drink?"

That caught the Imperial Consort's attention. Peeking over her shoulder she found the woman smiling and serene. She saw the stoneware cup. She wanted that water. "Yes."

Leaving her corner, Sigil padded to the counter. The cup was taken and brought to her lips. Once drained, she held it out so Elba might refill it. "Thank you."

"It's nothing."

"Elba..."

The baker set her work aside. "Yes, Quinn."

Hearing that name softened the severity of Sigil's frown. It softened her heart. "While you are at the palace, there is a high ranked woman charged with your care. Her name is Lady Belloy. My Jerla favored her. Do all she says, but watch what takes place around you. There is something about her... Something I can't put my finger on."

"I'll serve you as best I can."

Sigil picked up the nearby offering basket, handing it over to the older woman. "Now go. Herald Mathias is expecting you. He will oversee your transformation."

Elba was serene, as if all they conspired to do was nothing. She was tranquil; she was content.

Before the shop's door closed, Sigil added a troubled, "Don't die."

The baker smiled, and the door closed.

Uninvited, Sovereign put his arms around her, turning her head with a light touch. "She will be under the same guard charged with protecting you."

There was a brief shadow on Sigil's brow. "And I was struck in the chest with a missile."

Forehead to hers, the Emperor cupped her cheek, tracing her lips with his thumb. "I am sorry your Jerla was murdered, I am sorry you were harmed. It will not happen again."

There was no point in resisting his attentions, not after what had passed between them the night before. Not while he was giving her time to save the city.

She let him enfold her in a far too familiar scent, the heat of his body, and the immensity of his mind. Sigil even closed her eyes, almost enjoying the way the magnitude of him could separate her from everything else—outside emotions, her own feelings—until she was just a pinpoint. A solitary speck in an empty universe.

The Emperor pressed his lips to her temple and let her go. When his less than subtle mental manipulation ended, he put distance between their bodies, and she turned her head back to the window.

Her depression returned as if it had never abated.

Delight was rich in his voice, his temper mild, happy, and enticing. "Even with all this, with the loss of your Tessan boy, there is cause to be happy today."

Heartbreak lay heavy in her chest no matter how much Sovereign might think to dilute it with his *feelings*. Sigil was plagued with regret over Jerla, with loss, and personal culpability. Her fingers slid from the glass, puzzled that he'd dare make light of such a day. "What do I have to be happy for?"

"Because the thing you desired most, I have given you." He gave her a dazzlingly beautiful smile. "You're pregnant, beloved."

Her sigh was loud, it was aggravated, and it was full of warning that she had no stomach for his tricks. "Don't be ridiculous."

"Come now, precious Sigil." He reached out to toy with the lobe of her ear. "Don't you feel the shift in your chemistry? Have you not wondered why you do not feel well? It is as Karhl hoped. You were fertile when we shared you." He dared to palm her stomach, to box her in with muscled arms. "The pregnancy has been confirmed."

Sigil went stiff, not only from his touch, but from that intrusive *feeling* again. Like all the other emotions he'd purposely projected to influence her, she was saturated in his exaltation.

Though Sigil had known peace with Que, she had not known anything near what Sovereign held for her and for the baby he claimed lay in her womb. His overzealous pleasure was so vibrant, it was like an infection chewing at the edges of her rage.

It was worming its way inside.

"It's okay." Sovereign kept his voice low and sweet, cajoling. "I know you believed no child would be possible. So, until you accept that a perfect life is indeed inside you, I will carry the joy for both of us. I can show you how to feel it." He kissed her dirty fingers, a lingering soft thing before flooding her with an ocean of emotion. "See? This is love, this is what it feels like."

The idea of allowing such a consuming *infection* was appalling. Emotion of that nature was unreliable, compulsory on Sovereign's part, the very thing that controlled him and all the Brotherhood.

Que's species had known better.

But, the Axirlan had once told her that if he *could* love her, he would have. Que would have loved her. Sovereign *did* love her—chemically mandated love forced on the Brotherhood when they'd willingly swallowed her serum over a century ago.

Karhl loved her. Arden loved her. All of them loved her.

Except perhaps Tiburon… the one who helped her escape Condor. The one she'd scarred when they'd clashed in the Durazgabi system almost seventy years ago. The one who'd given her vials of his semen just so she might take a private tour of the capital. The one who promised he'd never lie to her.

"Beloved?"

Sovereign smelled of running water, of cooling ice, and night's sky. He was hauntingly beautiful, perfectly sculpted with eyes Sigil had openly admitted were pretty. So close, she looked over that face, over the face of the father of what he claimed was growing inside her.

He wanted a child, wanted it almost more than he wanted her.

Sigil did not mirror his delight. Under his infectious wonder, she felt her own itching dread.

Sovereign's hand slipped over her robes, fingers spreading to cup where their baby grew. "Now, our daughter is a small, delicate thing. In order to keep your word to me and save the Converts in this city, you must be careful with her. You'll have to control yourself."

"If I was really pregnant, you would never let me out of your ugly palace." Sigil was certain he must have thought she was incredibly stupid to think so obvious a trick might work. "Especially not to prance around in a sea of possibly hostile Converts."

Embracing her a little too tightly, Sovereign trilled his fingers against her belly. "It's safer for you if the Soshiia have no idea where you truly are. And I trust you to keep your word."

She wanted to bang her head against the glass, to shove him away and just *think* for a minute, but the man would not stop talking. Sovereign nibbled her neck, keeping her focused on him. "There is no reason to be scared." The palm of his hand wrapped the back of her skull, the man's expression gentle. "Imagine what our daughter will feel like moving inside you. Imagine how she'll look at you when you hold her to your breast. The Empire will nurture her;

your Brothers will love her. We will raise her, and with every subsequent sister you birth, her life will only grow more fulfilled."

Enough was enough.

She pushed him off, breaking Sovereign's hold and shattering a good deal of the painted pottery Elba had hanging from her wall. Once clear, Sigil's hands fisted and pressed to her temples. "Why are you telling me this now? Do you think I will give up my hunt? Do you think I will forget what you promised me?"

Sovereign seemed prepared for such an outburst. "You can be reckless with your body, Sigil, and there is great danger in the capital now. Our agreement stands. So long as you give me a child, I will not cleanse the city."

And there was the crux of his ploy.

Sigil stilled, pulled her fingers from the mess of her hair, and faced a warrior far stronger than she was. "Our agreement was that I would end the ones responsible for Jerla's death myself."

Sovereign shook his head. "You asked for the city to be spared in exchange for giving me a child."

"Don't do this to me, Sovereign!"

"You cannot go near them, precious Sigil. You have no idea what the Soshiia are capable of, what they might do."

"Of course I don't! How can I when not one of you will tell me what they are!"

"What they are doesn't matter. What matters is that you are pregnant. Think of the future of our child, I am begging you."

"Jerla was my child... and the Soshiia murdered him." Once the words were out of her mouth, Sigil stood stunned. Hearing it, seeing the little Tessan's ruined body at the moment of his death—the gruesome hole right between his shoulder blades. In the madness on the balcony, in her pain and shock, she had not noticed it, but *he* had been murdered. Whoever fired that missile had never been aiming for her heart; the Soshiia had been aiming for his. Otherwise he would have only lost an arm and the grisly hole would have broken through her chest.

Why?

Sigil took a seat on Elba's wooden bench. Gathering herself, she took a deep breath, and she looked deep into the growing dusk. The Fracturing would begin soon, it would seep through all survivors in the city, open them up and fold them together... making her pain disappear for only a moment.

Just like it had when the Soshiia had used the distraction to shoot a missile right into Jerla's heart.

Sigil was not going to stand for it. Sovereign's tricks, his deceit, his exploitations of her feelings and refusal to speak the truth—she would put a stop to all of it. "Do you remember what I did to Drinta? Did you see how easy it was for me to rip out her heart, tear off her head, and crush her bones into nothing? That is what I will do to the Soshiia."

Sovereign fell to his knees before her, gathering her hands in his. Earnest, he said, "Jerla is gone, Sigil. Our daughter is here. It is *she* who deserves your devotion now. He was a kind boy who would not want you to harm a baby on his behalf. Let your Brothers handle the Soshiia." He thought to be gentle by stroking her arms, by softly smiling. "We can go back to the Water Palace, you and me. No humans will trouble you there. We can spend our days in the seasons, making love, talking... Our baby could be born there."

"And who will run the Empire you built in my name? Who will herd your courtiers, the Brotherhood? Who will stop the Soshiia from continuing their corruption of your human drones?" There was no irresistible, furious need to hurt him. In that moment she was free of her indoctrination, thanks to the sperm still leaking down her thigh. There was only Sigil and cold honesty. "You can't find them, you can't sense them, and you can't track them. But I *can*. I will."

Sovereign was not to be moved. His smile fell, hardness taking its place as he opened negotiation. "What can I give you? I'll do anything."

Sigil put her hand to Sovereign's cheek, touching him as if not quite sure how to do it properly to show comfort. "Anything?"

"Yes." Though his voice was controlled, his answer was abrupt, hinging on frantic. "Anything you want!"

From her periphery, Sigil could see the beginning dazzling light of the Fracturing. The

Converts began their chant, the rich hum vibrating through the very stones of Irdesi Prime. Out in the square, far from where they sat, Elba stood in the place of the Imperial Consort, her people glorifying her, moved by the sight of their risen queen. But in the bakery it was only Sovereign and Sigil, a familial image polluted by too many agendas and too many years of accumulated loss.

"All I want is an answer." For the first time ever, Sigil dared to really look inside the man who loved her to the point of madness. It was like staring into the sun. It blinded, burned, and left a mark she could not unsee. But it was worth it. Under all Sovereign's artifice, hidden like a stain on dark clothes, at his very core he was absolutely wretched with guilt. "Sovereign, who are the Soshiia?"

As if he could feel him picking through mind, the man's lips parted, his face one of dread. "Stop."

Though he scrambled to cover, the tenor, the color of his emotions… for a few precious seconds, he could not hide from her.

Sigil knew his pain, because it was hers. She knew the kind of history that scarred a soul that deeply.

Seeing him bared, she felt her eyes prick, vision distorted by gathering tears. "You raped me on the floor of the home I shared with the man I loved. Karhl watched. That is how the Soshiia were created."

"You misunderstand..." Sovereign pressed his hand to where hers sought to leave his cheek. He held his face to her palm, eyes desperate. "We did not know you had conceived on Pax. We did everything we could to save them once your body began to abort. High Adherent Corths, in all his brilliance, is not Dr. Saniel." The Emperor looked openly despondent, his voice unsteady as he confessed. "It would have been better to let them go, but you were so damaged there was no assurance you would survive. You have to understand, what was done, was done out of love."

Sigil was hardly able to speak. "What was done?"

Sovereign rushed to explain, eyes wide and frightened. "Everything was provided for the twins: a loving home, safety, education. They wanted for nothing."

Those damaged little creatures who had been mangled by her violence and the Brotherhood's hurried attempt to patch them back together had not been raised by their own kind.

And now Sigil understood the slander, Unsalvageable. The Brotherhood did not see them as complete.

Sigil knew who it was, the human who'd been granted offspring with a remnant of Project Cataclysm—the old woman who'd worn a blue sash. The old woman Jerla had favored. "Lady Belloy—"

Cutting in, Sovereign assured, "Was a good mother. They had many happy years."

"Why didn't you tell me the truth? Why build a conspiracy and encourage me to chase my tail through books that would never mention something so shameful?”

“The truth? You wanted me to tell you that you ruined our firstborn children with radiation and lead?” Sovereign released a false laugh, yet looked as if he might weep. “I love you too much.”

They were surrounded by bread, baskets and baskets of it Elba had made ready so Sigil might search the square for the agents responsible for the death of her boy. All the work would be wasted, the food would spoil, and eventually, like Sigil’s heart, it would putrefy.

There would be no selling of bread in the square.

“Why did they kill Jerla?”

Sovereign could only conjecture. “Jealousy? Anger? They are not sound, Sigil. We don’t know why they turned.” He tried to wipe the tears from her face, but she wrenched her neck back no matter how he thought to soothe. “Understand that they are dangerous, that they are capable, and that they are here to cause you harm. Do not repeat the mistakes of fifty years ago by risking the little life inside of you.”

With that, Sigil started sobbing. “Everything I touch rots.”

“None of us blame you.” Eager to end her crying, Sovereign implored, “You must know that.”

Guilt and shame, were not foreign feelings— they were what Sigil was crafted from. She was pure in that sense, unwilling to pretend differently. “Of course you do. That’s why you’ve done all of this. It’s why you lock me up, why you watch me. It's why there is an implant in my brain."

"You did not know you were pregnant. Even we didn't notice until you began to bleed." Gripping her robes, touching and patting and doing all the things a human might do to comfort another, Sovereign tried to urge her understanding and acceptance. "You are free of the compulsion now. You are healing from the effects of Condor. You are where you belong, and the Soshiia will be put where they belong."

"Back with Lady Belloy? Locked in a pretty palace surrounded by water?"

Sovereign shook his head. "No."

"In prison?"

"You're missing the point. They are not your children. They never were." He watched her, kept his arms around her, and opened up his mind to tempt her to feel that all he said was true. "Too much was done when your womb forced them out. They are too different. They are not one of us. They were not even born of your body."

"Does Lady Belloy know what she carried? What she raised?"

"No. Matron Delphine is under the impression her daughters thrive serving the conversion effort galaxies away from here." Sovereign offered a shaky smile, holding her eyes as he promised, "Believe me when I tell you that she is a good woman, that she loves them."

Watching the man kneeling at her feet, at the indomitable master of the empire, Sigil found Sovereign's pain endearing in the most awful of ways. "Which is why you had the old woman dragged here. These Soshiia twins are fond of her. You don't believe they'd harm the one who raised them. So you kept Lady Belloy near me, near Jerla..."

"Do not fault me for taking precautions against an insidious enemy. They prey on our people, manipulate and destroy. Decades ago, one of them made it near enough to disturb you in cryo. They cut off your hands, Sigil. Took your eyes, your hair. They broke your jaw, knocked out several of your teeth... It was as if they had been stomping on your head."

How familiar...

The question little more than a breath, Sigil demanded to know, "What are their names?"

Voice thick with feeling, Sovereign put his head to her chest, the man looking for comfort just as much as he was looking to hold her still. "I love you... this changes nothing."

Beyond the pressure of his embrace, there was this weight on her chest, this great horrible feeling. "I know you do."

He put a hand to the back of her neck. He pulled her in for a kiss, promising, "I will make this right."

Sigil closed her eyes when their lips brushed, she felt the slide of his mouth over hers, his regrets, and how much pain he could no longer hide behind his mask.

Before he might sense her intention, the meat of her palm shot straight up and caught him under the chin. She struck with such force his neck snapped back, bones broken, her momentum taking them both to the floor.

They fell in a heap.

Just like the last time she'd brought him low, Sigil stood over her prey and met his frantic eyes. "You cannot make this right, but I can." Silently, efficiently, she shattered his legs and arms, before pulling her pilgrim's hood over her hair and face. "Goodbye, Sovereign."

Chapter 14

"Well done, Sovereign." Tiburon sauntered forward, coming to stand where the Emperor gripped the palace balustrade.

His leader glared as the masses scattered now that the evening's Fracturing had ended. "Mission report."

Grinning, chipped teeth on display, Tiburon laid the mockery on thick. "You give Sigil too little credit. In four days we've already found three mutilated bodies tossed aside on the street. How many agents do you think she's murdered that we haven't found? I don't see any reason to pester her when she's doing a better job of resolving the problem than you ever did."

In a blur, the Emperor held Tiburon by the neck, the Lord Commander's toes hardly scratching the floor. "You give me nothing of worth, while she is out there alone."

The weight of a heavy hand came to rest of Sovereign's shoulder, Karhl urging him to release their Brother. "Sigil may be watching. Is this what you'd have her see?"

Dropping the ever aggravating Tiburon, Sovereign heeded Karhl's warning.

Before Tiburon had fully found his feet, the Lord Commander drew back his lips and snarled, "Be careful, Sovereign. If you want her back, you need me. I'm the only one of the Brotherhood she trusts."

The nastiness of Sovereign's laugh was nothing to the hate in his eyes. "You always imagined yourself to be greater than you are."

Cracking his neck, Tiburon let his disgust, his scorn, lay open in his expression for every Brother on that balcony to witness. "She'll never come to you, not now that she knows what you did." He pointed to Karhl. "Just as she'll never go to him willingly again. She wanted to trust you, Karhl. I think she may even have cared for you. She won't anymore."

White hair chimed, Karhl shook his head in deep disapproval. "Careful, Tiburon. You cannot stand against us both."

Tiburon's eyes swept over his collected species, at the sorry remains of what had once been a vast and terrible force, shouting so every last damn one of them would hear. "Sigil is faithful to those who have earned her trust—more faithful than you can imagine! You see"—eyes greener than envy snapped right to the leader of his kind—"I was the one who told her how to escape from Condor. Just as I helped her escape the Durazgabi system by sacrificing my fleet and my face, before *you* might reach her."

"WHAT?" The balcony shook, Sovereign crushing the marble balustrade to powder under his grip.

Before the Emperor might strike, before Karhl might tear him in half, Tiburon let a grin break across his face. "For almost a century, I've known exactly where she was and who she was with."

The Emperor roared, the man's eyes wild as he gathered psionics powerful enough to bring down the palace if allowed to rage uncontrolled.

There was a change in his face, Tiburon showing an anger darker than black. "She was happy, Sovereign! The Axirlan saved our girl, he adored her, helped her, taught her, raised her. She was *happy* until you barged in and took all she'd worked so hard to achieve. Like Arden, you are selfish, impatient, and unworthy." In that moment, Tiburon looked old. Old, wise, grisly, and unrepentant. "Even without having choked down her serum, I loved her enough to leave her alone!"

Sovereign was not moved. "You will suffer for this betrayal, for all the Brothers who died searching for our wounded female."

Tiburon was not done. The furious warrior stalking forward to bellow right in the face of the galaxy's greatest terror. "Her Que would have died of old age had you waited! What was another hundred years when we controlled so much of the known universe? What was a hundred years compared to her joy? You could have brought her here gently had you not been so self-consumed."

Sovereign flat-out laughed. "And let her rampage through the galaxy when the alien was no longer able to control her? Did you not see the damage she caused herself on Pax? There were no guarantees a life left in that hellhole would have continued smoothly. She's safe here!"

"Safe?" Tiburon scoffed, gesturing to the very spot their female had almost been blown in half. "Since you've touched her life, she is constantly miserable, friendless, and terrified. You take and take and force and twist and lie. And what have those lies achieved? She's gone, Sovereign, hunting her mutilated children because you couldn't bring yourself to kill them when you should have!"

Sovereign struck the man with the force of his pent up fury, Tiburon's armored body flattened to the ground by psionics that would have left a human nothing more than pulp. Cold, dark, and eager for blood, the Emperor walked over to his struggling victim and sneered. "You would dare?"

Spitting out a bloody tooth, Tiburon gave all he had to fight the force of powerful psionics, to turn his head under the monumental strain and look his attacker in the eye. "Now you seek to defend the girls? Are they Unsalvageable or aren't they? You can't have it both ways. They are your children or they are Soshiia: *half-formed.*"

Karhl crouched down with questions of his own. "Have you been in contact with Maylin and Vara? Do you know where they are?"

The weight of Sovereign's power made it difficult for Tiburon to breathe, still the Lord Commander managed to roll on his back and chuckle. "I know who does."

Sovereign cast his shadow over the man. "Enough games, Tiburon."

"Arden knows where they are." No playfulness, no mockery, and no meanness colored Tiburon's reply. "He is here, right now, in the city."

"That isn't possible." Sovereign scowled and his eyes grew glassy, as if running the probability of such a scenario through his head. "No ship could have made it through the blockade."

Losing the ability to breathe under such weight, Tiburon coughed and fought to say, "No Imperial ship. But with a cloaked Tessan vessel, your snake would know just how to creep into the garden."

The Emperor set a boot to his most hated Brother's chest.

Even as Tiburon's ribs began to crack, as blood began to drip from his mouth, he laughed. "I raised you, Sovereign, trained you. You are my Brother and an old part of me might even consider you my son. But Sigil gave me the means to finally slaughter Dr. Saniel. For that, I would die for her long before I would die for you."

Sovereign pulled his mouth into a sneer. "You're not dying for me, or for her. You're just dying."

"Enough, Sovereign." Karhl stood tall, forcing his bulk between the Emperor and his prey. "If what the Lord Commander claims is true, Arden's plots may be a greater threat than the Soshiia. I do not believe this Brother would lie." Icy eyes glared down at the sputtering man at his feet. "That is not how Tiburon operates."

Removing his foot from Tiburon's chest, Sovereign kneeled, peeling his inferior's head from the ground. He looked dead into the eyes of the Brother who had taught him to lead, the Brother from whom he had taken the title Sovereign… the Brother he hated most, and swore, "Sigil will not be able to save you from me when this is over."

When crushing psionics let up, Tiburon threw off the Emperor's touch and struggled to stand. "And who is going to save you from Sigil once Arden gets his claws into her? Your judgment cannot be changed, so long as you live, he can never have her. He'll deactivate her implant, convince her to kill you." Bloody teeth on full display, Tiburon gave the meanest of grins. "You should be thanking me for saving you from your own blindness, my boy."

It was just like Pax. He had been playing a game with her, popping in and out of her awareness like a ghost, winking from a corner, only to vanish—brushing a kiss to her cheek when she stalked through the crowd to have her turn on him and find nothing but shadow.

Arden was haunting her.

It had been going on for days, Sigil sensing him but unsure of exactly where he was. At first she'd thought the Brotherhood was about to descend upon her. She'd pulled a knife, fingered a stolen plasma blaster strapped to her hip.

...and then nothing.

A few moments later, Sigil scented another Soshiia, all thoughts of Arden forgotten. She'd found the *Unsalvageable* peppered in crowds, snatching them up from the masses like a bird of prey. Mostly she went unseen, those around her unaware the body glued to her side, the one with an arm over her shoulder was either already dead or suffering greatly.

Useful psionics, that's what Sovereign had called them, were much, *much* more than useful. Her applications had been graceless at the beginning, but now, Sigil could tease a corpse to look like it walked. She could gently manipulate objects, even people, with a light touch she'd never been able to master as a child.

Stacked against her enemy, against the Soshiia's mutated Converts, she felt powerful. And it felt good to hunt.

She almost felt free.

But then there would be a flash of the golden one.

Lifting her head, licking coppery blood from her lips, Sigil knew he was near.

On the ground before her was another of the dead. Fresh meat she used to fortify her body. There was something about every Unsalvageable she'd tasted. They were all sweet, familiar.

They tasted a little bit like Sovereign.

Sigil had been gorging herself on the sorry fools.

Pinky finger between her lips, picking out a piece of meat stuck between her teeth, Sigil sat back on her heels and perked her ears. Yes, Arden was there, she could hear his mind, his gentle offer of non-violence.

"If you only knew what I risked to come to you."

It was the first time in five days Sigil had heard him dare to speak. Immediately she pinpointed the slip of shadow he thought to hide in, smiling so he could see her blood stained gums. "You are supposed to be fawning all over the Tessan Authority. Did Sovereign bring you back to tempt me home?"

One step out of the dark, half his body still shadowed, Arden exposed himself. "You know he didn't. I had been ordered away from you. As it was, it could have been decades before I saw you again."

Wiping her mouth on her sleeve, Sigil stood, her meal only half finished. "But here you are."

There was a flash in Arden's golden eyes. "It's *how* he orders that dictates what I can and cannot do. For those of us willing to risk ourselves, there are ways around his unmitigated influence."

Cracking her neck in preparation of combat, Sigil smiled. "And what was his exact order?"

Arden lifted his arms, showing her his hands were empty, that he was unarmed and at her mercy. "Understand there is so much I want to tell you, so much I wish you knew, but I cannot physically form the words you need to hear. Had Sovereign been more thorough when he'd commanded me to leave you, had he said, 'never see her again,' I would have had to approach you with my eyes closed."

Tiburon had said something like this when they'd clashed in the pub weeks ago. It was a conversation Sigil had thought over many times in the last few days, sitting with the remaining vials of semen he'd given her held tightly in her fist. The scarred Lord Commander had brought up the concept of her children in parameters that were inaccurate but telling. He'd planted the seed, he'd tried to communicate with her the way the two of them spoke best—through threats and violence.

Toeing the corpse at her feet, pushing it aside to clear the way, Sigil said, "And here you are, interrupting my lunch."

Braving a few steps closer, Arden offered everything he was. "Sweet Sister, let me help you."

Arden lacked Sovereign's emotional cloaks. Looking into him was unsophisticated and almost comforting. The Herald was not lying, but that didn't mean he was telling the truth. It was as he'd claimed. It's how one sculpted perception and reality.

Sigil did not trust him at all. "And just how would you do that?"

Arden swallowed, visibly tense. "You must figure out who *they* are. I cannot say it—I can't write it. I can't tell you, but you know! My journals were full of hints: when their uprising began. How the Unsalvageable, their agents, are corrupted. There is only one way such a thing could happen."

Sigil had no interest in remaining unprotected where the Brotherhood might find her. She had no interest in distractions from the sly Herald. "By another female of our kind. I know."

"And therein lies the complication." Arden held her eyes, earnest for her to understand. "The Soshiia are not other females."

Eyes narrowed dangerously thin, Sigil hissed, "They are my daughters. Sovereign told me what was done."

Arden did not say a word, but he looked very much as if he wanted to.

Sigil could play the roundabout guessing game. She filled in the blanks. "Who were altered by High Adherent Corths when he found the embryos damaged."

Arden's eyes got wider, urging her to continue. His words were carefully chosen, picked one at a time as if looking for the right puzzle pieces to craft a sentence that might guide her. "And how would he do what you propose?"

Her expression grew internally focused, as if Sigil were conducting some great mental mathematics. "You lack the technology to clone me, otherwise there would be many copies. Sovereign also swore he'd never do such a thing. I believe him."

"*He* didn't, and we can't."

Arden was wasting her time, Sigil's impatience obvious. "I don't fault High Adherent Corths for trying to save the daughters I'd ruined. If he took cells from me to patch them, he would have had my thanks."

Arden shook his head as if to warn her. "Keep that in mind when you meet them."

Sigil abandoned her meal for a new offering, her hand reaching out to take Arden's arm in her grip. "You know where they are? You know how to end this?"

He could not have looked more relieved to have her close, to feel her touch, even if her fingers squeezed to the point his bones ached. "All they want is to set your Brothers free from Sovereign's influence. We are his slaves."

Chapter 15

Arden was in a great deal of pain. Whatever he'd anticipated, what he'd hoped for, Sigil had not supplied. She had her own accounting, and it would seem the Imperial Consort found him liable.

Or she was just bored.

Wheezing for breath, he watched her toy with an empty glass cylinder, her eyes distant as she rested against the wall.

They were alone, just the two of them in her newly commandeered hovel. Every day she dragged him someplace different, every day she ate another part of him, while he screamed behind her palm.

She'd sleep with his torso serving as her pillow.

"What are those?"

Snapped out of her daydream, Sigil looked at the broken man, at the stump of his left arm and the remnant of his right leg, licking her lips. "These"— her fist closed tightly around the vials—"are the reason you have survived my companionship for the last three days."

In fact, though she was the cause of his misery, she was also the one who held water to his lips, who brought him food so he might regenerate. She even cleaned his wounds once her teeth were done ripping muscle from his bones.

"What you need from me is not sustenance." Arden forced his broken body to sit up taller, to uncurl. "How long has it been since a Brother has been inside you?"

She actually laughed, even if it was a soft, almost silent thing. "In your current state, do you really think you might perform? You are practically bloodless. You can't walk. You can't fight. How in the world would you survive being fucked by me?"

It was as if his pain was gone, the man soldiering to attention. "Then why keep me alive?"

An eye cold as ice winked. "I like you, Arden."

"And I love you."

Placing the vials carefully back inside her robes, Sigil leaned back against the stone wall. She let her hand rest on her stomach and eyeballed her captive as if tempted to feast. "Are you aware that Sovereign believes I am pregnant?"

"Sigil." Arden tried to reach for her, his body slumping as he squirmed close enough to brush his fingertips against her leg. "That is wonderful!"

Such hope bloomed in the male, such joy, that Sigil let him have his moment. She let him touch her, his shaking fingers reaching to feel her flat belly.

Even wan, pale, and drained, Arden's smile was beautiful. "That is why you are so hungry, why you do not risk stealing food from the markets or dwellings."

It was odd feeling his tentative fingers press to her stomach. Odd and unwelcome. "I steal food to feed you."

As if enlightened to the secrets of the universe, the man nodded. "Just enough to go unnoticed. Just enough to keep us both alive."

She let him believe his flesh was some greater sacrifice. It wasn't.

"Do you feel her in there?" The man was taken with the little life, his body slumping until he might rest his head in Sigil's lap. "Can you sense her?"

"My mother used to sing to me."

"The Kilactarin birthing tube?"

Sigil let him hear that his assessment of her mother, calling her a birthing tube, had caused offense in her harsh reply. "It was constant. She focused all of her attention on me when she had the faculty to do it. I always knew she was there—even when I was in great pain, when I was lonely, when I lacked hope."

He let his head fall into her lap, lying back as if they were intimates, as if he trusted she would never hurt him. "Are you singing for her now?"

"Something like that." Sigil let her hands play in Arden's long, tangled hair, her fist growing tight near his scalp. When she had a firm hold on him, she leaned down and showed her teeth. "And every time you speak, you interrupt my focus. Tell me, Arden, how will they hear me if my song is thready and weak?"

It was not the pain of her pulling his hair that drained the joy from his face, it was her intent. "Is this why you've moved us every night to a different quadrant of the city? The Soshiia? I know how to find them; you don't need to draw them to you."

"Oh, but I do." Sigil felt it even as Arden tried to bury such a feeling. The Herald was frightened.

"I don't think that's wise, Sigil."

Loosening her grip on his hair, Sigil hushed him, gently stroking his face as if she cared. "What is unwise would be to follow anywhere you want to take me. I trusted you once, and now I am here, Pax is gone, and Que is dead."

Golden eyes wide, Arden wrapped his only arm around her as if seeking comfort. "Please do not draw them here. I am begging you."

Sigil smiled softly. "I can feel them edging closer, toeing the line, unpracticed and unable to decide if they should cross it. It won't be long now."

The Herald was shaking, pushing at her as if to force her away. "You need to run, Sigil. Leave me here and run."

Easily catching his arm, Sigil pinned it to his chest. The way she grinned, the way she laughed, was terrifying. "And where would I run? To Sovereign?"

"I have a ship, a Tessan model with advanced cloaking abilities. Take it, go anywhere you wish."

"You were cleverer when you had all your limbs." She shoved him to the floor, kicking him away by the stump of his shoulder. "I would not last a month alone in space with no Brother to keep my mind steady."

"THEN TAKE ME! Gnaw on me day and night if you must, but RUN NOW!"

Getting to her feet, arching her back like a stretching cat, Sigil cooed, "And here I thought you were going to take me to them yourself. Why now don't you believe a meeting is such a good idea? It's not very nice to think so lowly of my daughters."

"That's not what they are."

It did not take her long to straighten her robes, to cease with her mocking and her play. Sigil grew serious, her eyes threatening murder. "I know exactly what they are."

She was already out the door, Arden calling after her. "PLEASE! I didn't know you were pregnant. YOU CAN'T! You'll hurt her."

Sigil ignored him, his frantic pleading, his anguish, as she walked out onto the chosen place where the approach of the Soshiia would give her greatest advantage. The Herald's screaming would draw a crowd, and, in time, Brothers would look to interfere. Still, the Imperial Consort made no secret of where she stood. She even left her hair uncovered so it might shine in the dark like a beacon.

Her girls were coming.

They had to climb to reach the rooftop, arms hooked like spider legs, to pull their bodies higher. When the pair of them crested the rooftop to stand before their mother, Sigil forced herself to look at what had been created because she had been too selfish, too wild, and too evil.

Condor was bloated and orange, the atmosphere abnormally settled, the evening sky bright enough she could see her daughters clearly. Both of them looked like her, they looked like Sovereign, even if they did not look like each other. But there was something in the way their bodies were configured that hung unbalanced and awkward. A slight hunch in the back, shoulders that were uneven, as if the girls were half formed between human and Sudenovan.

Their necks were too long, or not long enough.

Dr. Saniel would have laughed to see such shoddy work. Then she would have killed them.

Even with the defects, the woman on the left was undoubtedly beautiful, staring back at her with the same icy eyes, the same cold calculation. Her sister was not as fortunate. Something had gone wrong with her face, leaving half of it distorted... as if her skull had begun to melt.

Behind them, still working their way up the building, were the last Unsalvageables in the city. Six tainted Converts come to stand guard over their would-be queens.

The misshapen one spoke, half her face showing curiosity, the other half hideous. "I told you she'd want us."

Sigil kept her face blank, her finger on the trigger of the plasma blaster hidden in her robes. "Which one of you killed Jerla?"

"Is that Arden we hear screaming?" Only menace rolled off the girl who stood as Sigil's reflection. The pretty one didn't care if she was wanted by the Imperial Consort. "We were not sure if he would find you, though he swore he could."

Sigil ignored the question. "Sovereign will arrive soon."

The pretty one stepped closer in her sudden wild-eyed eagerness. "And when he does, will you kill him as Arden promised?"

It drew out an honest smile, Sigil charmed. "I have met your mother, Lady Belloy. Jerla liked her very much."

Such hate twisted the pretty one's face, pain marring her sister's countenance in equal measure as she said, "The Tessan boy… is that all you can speak of?"

Speaking over her sister, the pretty one, hissed, "We gave the Herald the codes to shut off your implant. You owe it to us to end Sovereign and put us in our rightful place!"

"Is that what you want?"

"WHAT WE WANT? Where are our statues in the Adherents' Cathedral? Where is our recognition as your daughters? The Brotherhood ignores us!"

Sigil interrupted the pretty one, chiding, "If you continue to shout, they'll find us more quickly."

"We were cast aside!" The girl responded with venom, letting wrath pour out in jerking movement, in her screams. "Forced to live on a mud-covered planet as if we were human—kept from a seat at court, from you." Abject fury, made the pretty one hideous. "They call us *Soshiia*... half-formed. We are disregarded. We are scorned."

Enough. Sigil could hear the self-entitlement, the sounds of a child screaming to have its way, to have more. It was ultimately disappointing. "Sovereign provided you with a good life, a family unit, and your chance to make a mark on your species."

The pretty one smiled. "We did make a mark."

She let her words coil around them like razor wire. Sigil let them hear the disapproval in her voice. "You used an incomplete serum made from yourselves on innocent Converts, to what, stir up a civil war? An army of them could not have stood up against five of your Brothers. You would have torn apart planets. Already your antics have cost the lives of millions, led to volatility in the Empire that protects our species from extinction—the Empire that protected you."

Motioning toward her sister, the pretty one hissed, "For years Vara has tried to convince me you could be reasoned with. I knew she was wrong. If you were dead, we would be necessary. We would be respected." Raising her hands to gather cycling psionics, the girl showed just how much she could hate. "*We* were the firstborns and no Tessan plaything should have replaced—"

Sigil could see that her disfigured sister had noticed, that the one with the distorted face was already reaching out to warn her twin. But it was too late. Sigil was the superior warrior, had been modified and trained as her warped children never had. Her arm rose, her finger kissed the trigger, and the one with the pretty face didn't have a face anymore.

There was a scream of disbelief, the living twin falling to her knees to catch the headless body of her sister. "Why?"

Smoke came from the neck stump, Vara holding her hands to it, as if she might put her sister back together.

Sigil made herself witness the anguish, the pain, all of this mess born from her. It was like walking through hell, a living nightmare—but it had to be done. Seven steps and she stood over the only remaining Soshiia.

As if to offer pity, Sigil explained. "Child, through no fault of her own, she was infected with my madness."

The girl was sobbing, despair marking every word. "She was your daughter."

"No." Sigil took in the smell of burnt flesh, took in the carnage, and refused to feel. "She was *me*, and I deserve to die."

They were no longer alone, the Brotherhood teeming like ants raced up the walls, over the balconies. The sad remnants of the twins' Unsalvageable army had already been eaten up by the swarm. A single ship hovered above, its gate down, the Brothers inside shouting down to her to take their hands.

Sovereign raised himself to the roof, his shout so loud it cut through the girl's screams. "Sigil, you must not!"

She did it gently, resting a hand on the base of something that was half her child and half herself, just as she'd cupped the neck of her mother years ago after the crash. The compression of her fingers, the wrench required to completely sever the spinal cord was instantaneous. The one called Vara even had the gift of looking her mother in the eye, of projecting her feelings of betrayal as Sigil projected the very emotion Sovereign had taught her was love.

And then that girl too fell dead, the body headless like her sister's.

Standing there, towering over them Sigil lay down the misshapen daughter she'd never know, and made herself look at what she'd done. No mental rampage came, no loss of control, only detached clarity and the feel of Sovereign's arms coming to restrain her and drag her away.

There was chaos in those extended seconds, so many shouting. Sigil offered no resistance and no explanation. She could feel Sovereign weeping, knew without turning her head, that he looked at the girls she'd destroyed.

When they were at a distance, shots were fired. He fell to his knees, injured, taking her with him as the Brotherhood swarmed nearer to close around the pair.

Sigil's eyes traversed the crowd, settling on Tiburon. Anchoring her attention, he nodded, not in praise, but in understanding… a part of him even hinted at gratitude that she'd done what was best for them all—what they could not do themselves. The great beast at his side, the massive Karhl, did not reflect the sentiment. Like his counterpart, he stared, as if waiting for her to lose control—because there was some unseen problem.

Karhl raised his weapon, a plasma rifle so large a human male could never have lifted it, and he pointed it at the ship hovering above his female. He pointed it at his own Brothers.

She had not noticed any sound over Sovereign's desolation, but it was there… Arden was shouting down at her from the ship. "KILL HIM! You must kill him now while your implant is still offline! Save us all!"

That was why Tiburon did not want her to look away, the Lord Commander needed her to see him. He needed her to see only him so he might mouth the words. "It was Arden who killed Que."

Her emotionless control had been so precise, so cold and perfect any Axirlan would have approved. And then it was gone, snapped away from her because Tiburon *never lied*. At least not to her.

Head snapping back, Sigil looked at the ship and saw the golden one. The Herald used his psionics to forge a leg made of pure energy, a Brother she did not recognize helped to support his weight. Arden reached out to her, imploring for her to finish it and set them all free. "YOU MUST KILL HIM NOW!"

It rolled through her, a wave of something so far beyond pain that no language possessed a word for it. Sovereign sensed the change. He took a grip of her head, as if to wrench it from her shoulders as she had done to her half-formed child. Lips pressed to the shell of her ear, he began to rattle off a code, a mixture of sounds that was no tongue she knew. Her skull was on fire, but physical pain could not register beyond the wrath eating her up inside.

Arden saw her face, Sigil's frosty eyes brimming with rage, and took a stuttering step back. Breaking her arm free of Sovereign's hold, her hand shot forward. She locked her psionics onto the ship, intent on pulling it down right upon her head—so that as Arden was crushed and burned she would see it, feel it, and relish her own bones breaking.

All Brothers on board began to panic, several pulled from their perch on the open gangplank only to fall and be destroyed by their own kind. The door's mechanics began failing, the ship's boosters firing up to fight the sudden loss of gravity.

She almost had them. She almost pulled that ship from the sky.

She would have, had Sovereign not spoken the final words, had her implant not come online to squelch her true power.

Like a fraying tether, her hold on the ship weakened, twisted, and snapped.

Arden and the traitors with him jumped into hyperspace before even clearing the atmosphere.

Their course had already been plotted, their plan for immediate escape in place—because they had planned to take her away… so she might be coupled with a new Sovereign, tied to a new group of males who would keep her to themselves no matter the consequences to the Empire or Convert humans.

The light of the ship's drive faded, Sigil lying in Sovereign's arms, covered in the blood of her children, and trying to fight him off like a madwoman.

"Hush, beloved. It's over now."

Even lost in his own pain, grieving that he had not arrived in time to prevent what Sigil had done, Sovereign fought to draw her back. It was not a quick transition from insanity to lucidity, but it was an agonizing one. When she could no longer fight, Sigil found her arms were fast around Sovereign, that she was howling a dirge into his shoulder as he rocked her and let her cry.

Chapter 16

Tiburon stood, hands resting on the marble balustrade, his eyes turned downward to the lower balcony where their species' sole female lay in a brief moment of sun. By the way her body draped over the settee, she was deep in sleep, her head resting on Karhl's lap. Nearby, trying to remain unobtrusive, High Adherent Corths scanned her growing belly, making notes on his handheld equipment.

Many of her Brothers had taken residence in the halls. They converged around her, more and more of the males arriving from distant planets the further her pregnancy progressed.

Every last one of them would be on Irdesi Prime for the birth. All of them had a right to see this new life.

Lord Commander Karhl fiddled with Sigil's hair, braiding and unbraiding bits of it, weaving in the chimes he wore in his own white mane. For a man who was harder than rock, he seemed tamed and contented… playful.

Seven months of Sigil's pregnancy had changed everything.

Tiburon had missed many of those months, having been in talks with the Tessan Authority and charged with commandeering Arden. Unfortunately, diplomacy could only go so far, and it was rare he was allowed to see her. "How is she today?"

"Better…" The question was begrudgingly answered by Sovereign as he stared down at the same scene. "Distant. Holding her attention can be difficult."

"When you speak so shallowly, my boy, it's like you don't know her at all." Pushing from the balustrade, Tiburon curled his lip and sneered. "Bring her a Kilactarin, bring her Elba, bring her the flesh of Arden for her to gnaw on, but do not expect her to enjoy your company."

The outburst was ignored, Sovereign enraptured by watching the way the wind tousled his female's gossamer garment. "Arden and those who absconded with him will be dealt with in due time. I will not bring an intergalactic war with a powerful species to our doorstep. I will not endanger either of them to end him quickly."

The Tessans were an older empire, with allies and alliances that could be called upon. There was no clear estimation of who would win a war of such magnitude. Both sides would be devastated. "You understand the gravity of this. There was an unprecedented fracture in our ranks. Our kind has never challenged the authority of the one who stands as Sovereign." It was rare for scorn to abandon Tiburon's voice, for censure to not hide between his words. He spoke plainly. He spoke as an old friend. "Without unity, all of us will die. How many here have let the idea of taking her for themselves cloud their judgment? How many will be patient to wait their turn while generations of daughters grow into adulthood?"

Cocking a brow, face stern, Sovereign darted a threatening glance to his predecessor. "You challenge my authority tirelessly."

The scarred one cocked his head, the metal filled wound down his cheek catching the light. "There is none more loyal in our family than I."

"We will not rehash old arguments now." Sovereign looked upon the Brother who had taught him to fight, where to strike... who had been Sovereign before him, and felt timeworn lingering animosity. "We coexist as we always have, because it is best for her."

As if the sleeping woman was in agreement, there was a grunt below them. Sigil flopped over, her arm thrown above her head. Below her breasts her belly protruded, round and hard.

Sovereign loved the sight, adored the woman, and desired greatly for things to be different. "Corths believes your presence is beneficial to the fetus. Sigil vomits less on days she interacts with you."

Tiburon lifted his chin, he smirked. "Because I let her gnaw on my forearm. She desires meat... yet you treat her like a human. She is far from human."

"She won't eat from me or Karhl. We've tried... and our younger Brothers... they might not survive her cravings."

"So I am to be her buffet? Tell the hellion I said no."

"I do not know what part of her blended DNA makes her this way. Is it the Sudenovan Matriarch, the Kilactarin? Is it the Gupp or the Tessan? The more her pregnancy advances, the less she can eat human food without growing ill.”

“We already knew she was a cannibal.” Tiburon laughed, tracing the metal line slashed across his face. “She was created to destroy us one way or another. Dr. Saniel was very thorough. When are you going to wrap your head around that?”

There would be no discussion on the matter. Sovereign was resolute. “You claim to love her. You will feed her. I will supply your wants in return.”

Tiburon looked at the Emperor, turning his body to lean lazily against the wall as he grinned. “I want her company tonight… in my rooms. We are not to be disturbed until I say we are done. If she wants, I will let her eat a whole limb.”

“I won’t subject her to your appetites.”

“Believe me”—an evil grin spread over the Lord Commander’s face, showing broken teeth and an unsettling excitement—“the brat enjoys my appetites.”

“Do not play games with me, Tiburon. When she leaves your rooms, she refuses to speak, sometimes for days.”

“So you send me on mission after mission off-world so she cannot seek me out. And it is *she* who comes to *me*.” Tiburon had earned her affection, held power in her regard. “She would sleep in my rooms every night if you did not interfere.”

Sovereign ground his teeth. “In order to maintain solidarity, she must be shared!”

"Yet you question what I do to her when we are together, why I refuse you access to my communications implant. When she's mine, she is mine alone." Tiburon would not be moved any more than Karhl would have been moved. "That is the way it is going to be, and you will accept it, boy."

Lips in a grim line, Sovereign demanded, "What is it that you do to her that I cannot see?"

Commands of this nature every Brother was compelled to follow. The Lord Commander had to answer—but the cat and mouse, the venom—Tiburon was at his finest. "We spend our time in conversation. We talk for hours, days, long past her need for sleep. She tells me everything: about Que, Pax, Condor, and all the other horrible places she haunted over the decades. I listen. I tell her the truth. That is what we do."

A rich, horrible envy bubbled up in the gut of the Emperor.

Tiburon was not lying... though Sovereign wished he were. He would rather have known the Lord Commander's cock was mercilessly invading Sigil's body than hear that Tiburon had successfully invaded her trust. "The hate I harbor for you, Tiburon, is fathomless."

"I would think you might hate Karhl more? Last I saw, he was doing things to your pregnant Consort you would hardly believe. The brute's whole fist was inside her... and she was begging for more."

The palace rocked on its foundation, Sovereign unable to contain such rage. "SILENCE!"

Below them Sigil was shaken from sleep, so startled she sat up, ready for battle, for bloodshed. Karhl was already trying to calm her, palming her belly and whispering at her ear.

It was not panic, exactly, that lay on her face, but it was a form of fear.

The greater her belly grew, the harder it was for her to move. The predator in her knew this. It made her cagey and eager to keep to the quiet and safety of her wing. Disturbing her was never a good idea.

There were hundreds of meters between them, yet Sovereign abandoned Tiburon on the balcony above and slid down the palace walls, landing in a hard crouch to be with her. As he straightened, he apologized. "I am sorry for waking you, beloved Sigil. I lost my temper."

The effect of his presence ran over her. Her eyes grew lidded, her breath soft. "Why? Has Tiburon returned? Have you news of Ard—"

No hesitation lay in Sovereign's psionic pull to drag her flush with his body. Before she might think on it, before she might yawn, he swept his tongue into Sigil's mouth. He wanted her drunk on the taste of him, trapped in that mental place where none other existed but the two of them. It was a power he'd had over her from the first, and one he would exercise mercilessly.

It was a power she had over him as well.

He projected intense love, she swallowed it down to fill her abyss—their mutual addiction satiated.

Tripping his fingers down her spine, his anger gone and his spite hidden from her senses, Sovereign looked down at his drowsy woman, at the chimes Karhl had woven into her hair, and smiled. "Tiburon has returned. Arden has integrated himself as a retainer to the Tessan Authority. He's maintaining political asylum. They will not extradite him. Assassination attempts will be met with 'equally appropriate aggression'."

Sigil looked uncertain, alternating between righteous anger and concern. "He thinks to shield himself from me by openly hiding behind a society I know better than this one, because he knows you will not risk the security of the Empire facing an opponent greater than floundering humans… not now that you have me, I am with child… and vulnerable. Arden has faith that you will keep him safe from me."

There were subtle ways to calm her beyond only pinching her neck. Sovereign put his hand on their baby, cocooning her with adoration. "Beloved, I would not risk war even if you did not carry our daughter. The Empire exists to provide you with security. Arden is not worth endangering that safety. The Tessans only use him to try to surpass our influence. The politics of the situation will run their course, then we strike."

She wanted to argue, hated Arden with such a passion that her hands trembled.

It had taken many long months before the Imperial Consort would even look at Sovereign or Karhl. After the deaths of Maylin and Vara, after Sigil learned the truth of what really happened on Pax, forgiveness for their culpability in Que's death, even if their part was unknowing, was not something she thought to ever extend. The fact that they had let Arden live all those years, even if he had been in a prison with nothing to do but write, even if he had been censured, disgusted her.

Knowing she had been left in his care day in and day out, burned her.

Both had arguments in defense of their actions. Sigil refused to listen.

Other Brothers were chosen to see to her *condition*, usually timid Corths, with his sweetness and gentle touch. If it was violence she craved, Admiral Parnisu and Admiral Gethman would come down from their ships and work together to overpower the testy woman.

Sovereign and Karhl were ignored, denied.

The child had a difference of opinion on the subject. Once the baby had developed to a point it possessed an early form of cognizance, it wanted Sovereign's constant presence. It wanted Karhl. It wanted peace.

Sigil did it for the girl, and in doing so, let them near again until both had become so ingrained in her life there was no undoing it. One of them was always with her, holding her, rubbing the small of her back.

She made herself grow comfortable in their presence, breathed slowly, and loved her unborn daughter past any point of collecting madness.

Sovereign had dominion over her now. She belonged to him. "His time will come, precious Sigil. Arden will make a mistake, expose himself to us. You will have him to do with as you will."

"Do not lie to me." She pushed him away, a trace of hurt twisted in her complaint. "You would never allow him to stand in my presence. You only say the things you think I want to hear."

Sovereign took her elbow, directing Sigil toward the door. "Let's go inside. We can talk. I will tell you anything you want to know."

She did not believe him, her opinion clear in her mangled expression. "Anything?"

If this was the way to make her love him, yes. "Anything."

"Let's start with the passcodes for every ship and byway in the Empire."

Cutting a worried eyes glance toward his stubborn female, Sovereign took a risk that might be the end of them all. He was honest.

In the months that slowly altered her body, Sigil found there was something ultimately fulfilling in brimming with life. Sure it was uncomfortable, her back always ached, she was always hungry, but her daughter was real, she was inside her...

Sigil had grown completely consumed by pregnancy.

Sovereign had been telling her of distant planets, their bizarre cultures, and the quality of Converts harvested from each.

Sigil's gaze grew far away… she was no longer paying attention. "What?"

Threading his fingers into the hair at her scalp, Sovereign leisurely ran his hand over their child. He kissed his Consort's forehead. "She must be awake. Does our daughter sing today?"

Settling against the father of her baby, Sigil took a deep breath and melted into perfect heat. "She does."

"What does she say?"

The baby didn't *say* things, only *felt* things, projecting them to the one who nourished her. "It is almost time."

The Brothers in the room perked their heads, Karhl daring a smirk.

It was not quite so precious a scene when her contractions began and Sigil writhed as if she'd not lived a life full of pain. Three full days of labor left her spent. None of her suffering mattered when Corths finally lifted a bloody squalling infant from between her spread thighs.

The High Adherent placed the baby on her breast even before the cord was cut or the placenta delivered. One long look at her, and a name was spoken no Brother in attendance dared to contradict.

Sigil named her daughter Que.

It was two weeks before she'd let one of the Brotherhood touch her, and then it was only because she was so tired, Sigil was afraid she would drop her. While the mother slept, every last Brother in the palace passed Que around. They counted her toes, her fingers, analyzed what might be the final shade of her eyes.

The Brotherhood's jubilation turned to concern—their Sigil did not wake, not for two days. When she did, she was confused, Sovereign by her side offering instant comfort by showing her their thriving baby.

Little lips were set to her breast, Sigil's nipple pulsating as the child fed.

Sovereign might stroke her hair, Karhl might pet her shoulder, Tiburon might have stood at the foot of her bed watching, but Sigil saw only Que.

Sigil didn't put her down for a year. For an entire year she smiled.

She adored the baby, even going so far once, and only once, to thank Sovereign for giving her so perfect a creation. Their female laughed and played. Once the babe was in her arms, she even spoke less of her intended revenge against Arden—of how she would hunt him down, tear apart the Tessan Empire that thought they could shield him—and eat him slowly.

But her fatigue grew, the baby was in her cradle the first time it happened. They found Sigil sprawled on the floor, Que wailing. She did not wake for several days, only to open her eyes unsure where she was.

Sovereign did not leave her side once.

Neither did Tiburon, which caused some tension.

When Que had started learning to stand, the mother could hardly stay awake, though she tried. With heartbreak, Sigil accepted the truth of the situation. They should have known this would happen. They should have been prepared. She was falling into another long sleep cycle, only this one was not plagued by madness, for the Brotherhood still saw to her sexual needs daily.

She was going to miss so much. She was going to have to leave her child in the care of the same men she would never fully be able to trust. She wept as she held her fair-haired daughter.

A few more cycles passed, Sigil moving slowly, and it happened again.

"It is time for me to sleep."

Sovereign assured her, seated next to her on the bed. "You are only tired because you try to carry the burden of the child's care alone. You need to rest."

There was pity in her wet eyes, pity that spoke of the honesty of her confession. "When you found me on Pax, I told you that decades of my lifetime I have slept. It was not a form of imprisonment forced upon me by Que. It was necessary rest. He watched over me. Had he lived, he would have urged me into cryo months ago. The signs are well-known to me."

Shaking his head, Sovereign stomached hearing of his long dead rival. "Corths will adjust your implant, my darling. If it is a question of chemistry, it will be resolved."

"Please… listen to me, Sovereign. It may be many years before I wake." Fear crept into her voice, it made her lip shake as she pleaded. She whispered to Sovereign that Elba was to care for her daughter. Que was not to be raised in the palace amongst the Brotherhood. They would taint her, Sigil insisted— indulge her too much, as the twins had been indulged. The girl needed to be taught humility, that she was a part of a whole.

The Imperial Consort made him swear using the only enticement she could. "I do know a fondness for you, Sovereign, for the daughter you've given me… I feel it here." She put her hand to her heart. "Love me in return. Promise me you'll do as I ask."

The man broke down, the palace quaking as he cried. He tried everything to keep her eyes open. He kissed her, thought to seduce with soft touches. He even screamed at her. "I cannot bear another forty-seven years without you!"

She did not twitch.

After many tests, Corths confirmed that Sigil was in some state of hibernation similar to her extended coma after the fall of Pax—and that there was nothing that could be done. She would wake up when she was ready.

It was Karhl who'd carried the toddler to the baker, Karhl who visited every chance he could. Que knew her father, she saw Sovereign often—the Emperor played with her, talked to her, but his heart was distracted, most of his hours spent underground tending to his sleeping Consort.

Tiburon hardly paid the girl any attention. Instead he ruled, unhappy with his lot to carry the weight of the Empire. Of all of them, Karhl suspected that it was Tiburon who missed her most.

Epilogue:

It was many steps down to the place the little one wanted to see. For years he'd carried her on his shoulders, or his hip for the visit. Not anymore. She'd reached an age where she no longer wanted help, not when she could show off how grown up she was.

Karhl held her hand, dwarfing her little fingers in his as she took the steps one at a time.

So far under Irdesi Prime's surface, they were surrounded by cool, constant atmosphere. It smelled of mineral damp, of unseen water, and the algae allowed to flourish so it might continuously purify the air.

There were still many steps to go, but the little girl began to grin. "She's singing today. No bad dreams."

Thank the gods. Not every visit was smooth. More than once, the child had grown frightened before she'd made it down the final steps. From the way the little girl had screamed, the terror in her voice, Sigil's occasional nightmares were truly awful.

The warrior composed his face into a small smile, completely taken with his companion. "Of course she sings. Your mother loves you."

For a second the little one grew sad. "Then why won't she wake up?"

"Come along, Que." Karhl carefully squeezed her fingers. "You don't want to keep her waiting."

The stairs curved again, and then a room full of soft light came into view. The tomb was a large one, the room's occupant lay upon a carved slab at the center. Around her, several soldiers stood still as stone, as if they too had been carved from the rock.

Releasing Karhl's fingers, Que ran forward with a laugh. "Look, Papa, Daddy's already been here today."

Under the fingers crossed over the woman's stomach sat a fruit with a dark purple rind.

Climbing on top of the display like a monkey, the little girl plopped down in the dreaming woman's lap. She took the fruit, and began to pick at the peel.

The Lord Commander moved to stand over them both. "Sovereign left that as a gift for your mother."

Impish, already stuffing mushed fruit in her mouth, Que said, "Mommy wouldn't care. She'd share if I wanted some."

A white brow cocked, Karhl remained unmoving. "And what will Elba say when you go home and have no appetite for dinner?"

That stopped little fingers covered with fruit pulp inches from the child's mouth. Que took the ruined thing, placing it back under her mother's fingers.

"That's a good girl."

Karhl turned his eyes from the child with pale hair just like her mother's so he might look upon the woman he loved. The back of his fingers ran down a cold cheek, the hulk bending forward to place a chaste kiss on Sigil's mouth.

For three years, he'd done so every day duty allowed him to linger on Irdesi Prime.

"You look sad." Sticky fingers wove into his, the little girl trying to comfort her favorite companion. "It's almost time for the Fracturing. It will make you feel better. I'll even hold your hand."

Lord Commander Karhl tore his eyes from the face of his sleeping lover. "I brought you here to show you something, child—something that does not make me sad at all."

That caught her interest. The little girl with eyes the green of seafoam sat forward, smiling brightly. "What?"

Above them the fracturing began, and though they could not see it, a dim reminder of the echoing connection could be felt deep underground.

Karhl laid his free hand over Sigil's, cocking his chin toward her face. "Look at your mother."

Que did as she was told, the stony face of the Imperial Consort altering so minutely a human would have missed it.

Sigil was softly smiling.

Just once the woman's chest expanded in a deeper breath, her child jostled.

The Fracturing ended, the smile faded, no matter how Que tried to press it back up with her little fingers.

Karhl put a reassuring hand on the child's back; he allowed inflection into his voice. "Your mother will wake soon."

To be continued...

Thank you for reading SOVEREIGN. Sigil's twisted story of love and redemption is far from over. QUE is coming soon! Make sure to sign up for my newsletter so you don't miss it!

Sign up for my newsletter 🐦

http://bit.ly/AddisonCainNewsletter

Addison Cain

USA TODAY bestselling author and Amazon Top 25 bestselling author, Addison Cain is best known for her dark romances, smoldering Omegaverse, and twisted alien worlds. Her antiheroes are not always redeemable, her lead females stand fierce, and nothing is ever as it seems.

Deep and sometimes heart wrenching, her books are not for the faint of heart. But they are just right for those who enjoy unapologetic bad boys, aggressive alphas, and a hint of violence in a kiss.

Visit her website: addisoncain.com

Sign up for my newsletter:

http://bit.ly/AddisonCainNewsletter

Amazon: amzn.to/2ryj4LH

Goodreads: www.goodreads.com/AddisonCain

Bookbub Deals: www.bookbub.com/authors/addison-cain

Facebook Author Page: www.facebook.com/AddisonlCain/
Addison Cain's Dark Longings Lounge Fan Group: www.facebook.com/groups/DarkLongingsLounge/

Don't miss these exciting titles by Addison Cain!

Omegaverse:
The Golden Line

The Alpha's Claim Series:
Born to be Bound
Born To Be Broken
Reborn
Stolen
Corrupted (coming soon)

Wren's Song Series:
Branded Captive
Silent Captive
Broken Captive
Ravaged Captive

The Irdesi Empire Series:
Sigil
Sovereign
Que (coming soon)

Cradle of Darkness
Catacombs
Cathedral
The Relic

A Trick of the Light Duet:

A Taste of Shine
A Shot in the Dark

Historical Romance:
Dark Side of the Sun

Horror:
The White Queen
Immaculate